# The Call of Duty

# The Call of Duty

Michael A. Diaz

**Writers Club Press**
San Jose  New York  Lincoln  Shanghai

**The Call of Duty**

All Rights Reserved © 2000 by Michael A. Diaz

No part of this book may be reproduced or transmitted in any form or by any means, graphic, electronic, or mechanical, including photocopying, recording, taping, or by any information storage retrieval system, without the permission in writing from the publisher.

Writers Club Press
an imprint of iUniverse.com, Inc.

For information address:
iUniverse.com, Inc.
620 North 48th Street, Suite 201
Lincoln, NE 68504-3467
www.iuniverse.com

ISBN: 0-595-12868-8

Printed in the United States of America

"What lies behind us
and what lies before us
are but tiny matters compared
to what lies within us"
Oliver Wendell Holmes, poet

This book is for
Colonel Ashley Brown
And
Charles Mann
Two of a kind

# 1

Part I
The Letter

Boston, Massachusetts
7 May 1973

    The heat wave consuming Boston was in its third day with temperatures in the high nineties again and the humidity almost a living thing. In May, the temperature should have been in the 70's, not in the 90's, but there it was and had been for three days in a row. The sky was cloudless, the late afternoon sun still retained most of the heat, making people walking the streets wish for rain or a slight breeze from the harbor to take away some of the incredible sultriness of the day.

    The few people who were on the streets walked fast, dashing into the restaurants and stores, searching for the coldness of the air-conditioning that they knew was there. It was a day to lay low or to spend it inside a cool place, drinking cold beer. But to the young man jogging down Cambridge Street in central Boston, laying low was the last thing on his mind. People looked at him running by and shook their heads at the crazy fool who was stupid enough to run downtown Boston in the middle of this heat wave. But the young man was oblivious to them, his long powerful legs eating up the distance easily. He was absorbed in his running, a crease etched deeply in his forehead. Looking at the man closely it could be seen that he was not breathing hard at all, his knees coming up high and his arms pumping rhythmically. The young man was Craig Barlow, 23 years old, and used to this. He had spent the last three years at Harvard on the cross-country team, excelling at the long distance races. He was a tall handsome looking man, with black curly hair and gray-green eyes that had a way of looking at life in a most cynical way for one so young. His face was long, almost aristocratic, giving the impression of strong character.

Despite the heat the young man ran efficiently, his chest rising and falling with each step. His skin shone with the sheen of sweat that covered his body, the droplets of sweat falling away as he ran, turning to sparkling diamonds in the sun. His body was hard and in the places where the sun had touched his skin it had a golden hue, deeply tanned, the muscles underneath his skin rolling smoothly with the effort of his stride. Dressed in nothing but a pair of black running shorts and a pair of Nikes, he cut a dashing figure in central Boston and more than one pair of female eyes followed his progress, admiring the young man's physique.

Running anywhere from five to ten miles per day, five days per week was his ritual, and on this particular Friday, he was into his fifth mile and almost home. He looked at the time on his Rolex sports watch and increased the tempo of his stride. He was running late and his fiancee would be pissed if she had to wait for him to get ready. They had a dinner engagement, a black tie affair that he didn't have any desire to attend, but knew that there was no way he could get out of it. His father, grandfather and his uncle would be there also and probably all the big names in banking and finance in the central Boston area. And his fiancee, Barbara Crawford, would not miss an occasion like this for anything in the world. Thinking about Barbara brought a frown to his face. For a man who's getting married in three weeks, Craig thought, I'm not having very good thoughts about my fiancee. At times like this he missed his mother greatly and wished that she were here to impart some sound judgment to his life like she use to. Catherine Weatherly-Barlow had died a year ago, after a protracted fight with brain cancer, leaving him and his father desolate. A week ago he had graduated Summa Cum Laude, obtaining his MBA from Harvard University Business School at the age of twenty-three. In another week he would be working for the family firm, side by side with his uncle and father. He had met Barbara two years ago while still at Harvard and at first he had fallen hard for her. She had been an ardent supporter of the peace movement and students against the Vietnam War and he had joined her, marching on campus and demonstrating against the war. Their numbers were not as great as they had been in the late sixties, but were still a force to be reckoned with by the political establishment. He had joined more as a way to get to know her than because of any deep ideals or concerns about the war. As far as he was concerned, Vietnam was a far away country that he would never see. It was just news on the TV for him and nothing more. Or at least he thought so, until the little speech given by his uncle, Henry Weatherly, one day at the dinner table. He had been running his mouth, talking about how the peace movement had brought the Johnson administration down and now they were about to do the same with Nixon. It was the waning days of the Vietnam War and everybody was sure that the war would be over by the end of the year and that Nixon would bring the rest of the 'boys' home. They had watched the CBS news with Walter Cronkite, his uncle's favorite commentator, and after that had proceeded to the dinner table where young Craig had started talking. The only other people present at the table were his father, Oliver Barlow, and his Uncle Henry and he had launched into an attack about the immorality of the war and the policies of the present Republican administration. His uncle and father had listened to him in silence until finally Uncle Henry had cleared his throat and fixed his pale blue eyes on him.

"Son", Uncle Henry said, his Boston accent clipped and precise, "I believe that in order for you to attack your government and its policies, or for that matter the war in Vietnam, you must earn the right to do so." He paused for a second, reaching for his napkin and dabbing at his lips carefully. Then he continued, his strong voice carrying easily across the room.

"And in order for you to earn the right, you must first pay the price." Craig Barlow heard the rebuke in his uncle's voice and was stung by it, and somewhat surprised at the intensity of the old man's feelings about the subject. "Uncle Henry, what are you talking about?" he replied, somewhat confused by the talk. "Earn the right? Pay the price?"

For a moment Henry Weatherly remained silent, his eyes clouded like he was a million miles away. Then he shook his head and continued talking. "If you want to disagree about your government and point out the things that you think are wrong with it, then you must pay the price first, Craig," he said, his voice clear and strong. "Otherwise you are just resting on somebody else's shoulders, getting a free ride."

"I'm sorry, Uncle Henry," Craig said, "but I'm confused."

Henry Weatherly got up from the table stiffly, a Scotch and soda in his hand. He was not a drinker, but allowed himself two of them in the evening with his meal. He walked with a noticeable limp on his right leg, the result of a bullet shattering his ankle during the Korean War and slowly, he approached Craig.

"Listen to me, son," he said, his voice now soft and kind. "I don't want you to be just like all the other long hair, rich, anti-establishment hippies who are out there cursing their government and the war without having any idea what it is they are protesting about." He took a sip of his drink and cleared his throat again. "They say they are protesting the war, but in reality what they are protesting is their fear of going to war, their fear of losing their deferment and of having to go and serve their country. Outwardly they say 'we want peace, end the war,' but inwardly, what they are saying is, 'let some other fool be the one to fight this war, let them die for their country.'" In reality, it seems to me that they don't have any idea what the words honor, country, and duty mean anymore." He walked stiffly back to his chair and sat down, taking a small sip of his drink. His brow creased in thought for a second, and then he continued.

"In order to protest you have to know first hand what you are protesting about and in order to do that, you must have paid the price." He got up again, feeling to restless to be seating, loosened his tie and paced the length of the dining room. Craig had stolen a glance at his father, noticing that he was listening intently to his brother-in-law. Oliver Barlow was fifty-one years old, a lawyer and had never served his country in any other capacity. He was a quiet, capable man and right now he was intrigued by his brother-in-law's dissertation.

"What I mean by earning the right to protest and by paying the price first Craig, is that the right is earned by shedding your blood, your sweat and your tears, either in war or in any other endeavor that serves your country," his uncle continued. "Then, and only then, have you earned the right to bad mouth your government and its policies. If you don't pay the price, then you are just enjoying the benefits that someone else paid for you, with their blood and probably with their life." He took another sip of his drink, paced the floor and then he stopped, fixing his eyes on Craig. Once again he continued, his forehead creased in thought. "A lot of people have talked about duty, honor, and country, but I don't believe that anyone has put it into words better than John F. Kennedy." He drained the Scotch, putting the glass down on the table. "By God, I hated his policies," he said with a chuckle, "but I have to admire his guts even if he was a Democrat. He said, and I quote, 'Ask not what your country can do for you, ask what you can do for your country'. There is more in those words than anyone can imagine son, all you have to do is think about them." His uncle had stopped then, the faraway look in his eyes again and slowly he walked away, the limp making a soft sound against the marble floor.

He had thought about those words for a long time afterwards, mulling their meaning over in his mind. He loved his uncle dearly and would not do anything to intentionally hurt him and somehow, he knew that what he thought about the war and duty, honor and country was important to his uncle. He had never returned to the peace movement after that and then, in March 1973, the war was finally over and he never thought about the "speech" again.

Barbara had been mad at him for quitting the movement, but he felt that it was the right thing to do and stuck to it.

She had played hard to catch, refusing to go out with him until suddenly, one evening, she had come to him asking if he was connected to the investment bankers, Weatherly, Weatherly and Barlow, Inc. The question had surprised him but when he answered in the affirmative, he had seen her face light up and her eyes open wide. Even now he could swear that he had seen a speculative look in her eyes. And after he told her that he was the grandson of Robert Weatherly, III, and the son of Oliver Barlow, she was almost beside herself. She had talked for what seemed to him quite a long time about his family and the fact that just about everyone who was anyone in Boston's society and the business community knew about the Weatherly investment bankers. A smile had flickered on Craig Barlow's face upon hearing that. He had known all his life that his family was rich, not just wealthy, but rich and that they had been in the banking business for over a hundred years. Later on he had found out that her family was in real estate and that they had done business with the bank on numerous occasions. After that the woman who had refused to go out with him for almost a month, couldn't get enough of him, whining and complaining when he couldn't see her every day and finally moving in with him, much to his chagrin. At first sex was great or at least he thought it was, until Craig came to the realization that Barbara was faking it most of the time. Under all the passion and desire that she displayed while they were having sex, the brain of a very cold and calculating woman was at work. The longer they stayed together the more he learned about her and the more reluctant he was about the wedding looming closer and closer on the horizon. The invitations had been sent and Barbara's family were busy making the thousand and one preparations, getting everything ready for the "big day", as his future mother-in-law was fond of calling it.

Turning into Tremont Street he looked at his watch again, calculating that he would make it to the loft that he called home in about two more minutes. The loft had been a birthday gift from his father, Oliver Barlow, in his third year at Harvard and with the help of a contractor who did business with Weatherly, Weatherly & Barlow, Inc., the place had been transformed into a very livable apartment. The fact that the bank had owned the entire block was not lost on Barbara either when she found out where the place was. In what he considered a weak moment, after making love to her until his whole being was satiated and his brain was 'mushy', as he put it, he had given her a key to the place. Slowly she had moved clothes and this and that into the apartment until eventually she was living with him. It had been done so smoothly and gradually that she was practically living with him before he even realized that she had moved in permanently. One more time he felt that Barbara Crawford had out maneuvered him.

He shook his head to get rid of the unpleasant thoughts and came to a stop in front of an imposing brick building. His place was upstairs while the downstairs was leased as a warehouse for a downtown business. Slowly he walked to a mailbox in place on the wall of the building facing the street and taking a key from a small pocket in his shorts opened the door to it, retrieving a pack of letters and magazines from it. Walking to the rear of the building he scanned the contents of the mail quickly. There were several letters for Barbara, the usual junk mail, invitations and letters from businesses and then he came across a letter in an oversized envelope. He looked at the address on the left-hand corner—The Pentagon, Washington, DC. Looking at the envelope Craig Barlow stopped on his way up to his apartment, a puzzled look etched on his face.

"What in the hell does the Pentagon want with me," he murmured, resuming his ascent to the apartment. He thought about opening the damn thing, but another look at his watch confirmed that he was late. Opening the door to the apartment he walked in, throwing the bundle of mail on the coffee table. The place was spotless, not a speck of dust anywhere or anything out of place. The loft consisted of two bedrooms, a small kitchen and living room and a bath, all furnished appropriately with the latest contemporary furniture. Barbara was a compulsive cleaner, always fussing about the place, complaining when he let his dirty clothes pile up in a corner or dishes in the sink. The damn place looks like nobody lives here, Craig thought, walking toward their bedroom, thinking that they might as well be married, the way she acted all the time. He opened the door and walked in, and his breath caught in his throat at the sight of the naked woman sitting in front of the bedroom mirror, applying makeup. Damn, but she was one beautiful woman, Craig thought, his eyes drinking in the loveliness of her.

Barbara Crawford was a tall woman, twenty-three years old, with long, shiny blond hair cascading down her back. Her eyes were green, reminding him of the color of the sea when a storm was approaching. Her skin was deeply tanned and had the healthy glow of youth. Her breasts were large, standing erect and proud, the nipples a shade darker than her tanned skin. Looking at the naked woman Craig's reaction was instantaneous, his erection overpowering in its intensity, threatening to come out of his shorts. Being a healthy and horny young man, Craig took a step toward Barbara, his eyes glued to her buttocks, a grin on his young face, his hand extended to grab one of her breasts. He had barely started to move when he heard Barbara's voice, cold as ice, directed at him.

"Craig Barlow," she said, her voice loud, almost shrill, rising slightly from the seat in order to look at him, "Don't you dare touch me. You are sweating like a pig and you—you stink," she added, her nose wrinkling in distaste at the odor emanating from him.

Caught in mid-stride, Craig stopped and looked at her, his erection going flat, his face showing the hurt that her words had produced. Seeing the look on his face, Barbara realized that she had been too abrupt with him and immediately put a smile on her face.

"We are running late dear, but I promise you that tonight we will have time for anything you want to do."

Listening to her words Craig's face lit up and he smiled.

"I'll hold you to that," he said, stopping behind her. He looked at her reflection in the mirror, his eyes lingering on her breasts and then, shaking his head, he walked into the bathroom.

# 2

He woke up with a start, the sound of the alarm next to his head making him jump. He reached for it quickly, glancing at Barbara sleeping next to him, punching the button to silence the damn thing. Barbara mumbled something in her sleep and rolled over onto her stomach, snoring softly again. He got up quietly, glancing at the clock again. It was five thirty in the morning, Saturday and today was his ten-mile run.ABathering his shoes, shorts and sweatband, he started toward the bathroom, his head throbbing slightly from last night's party. He drank too much and had stayed up later than usual, but he had to admit he had enjoyed himself. The party had been pretty much what he expected, a gathering of the rich, serving a good cause. The affair was an effort to raise money for children with cancer and apparently it had been a tremendous success.

He brushed his teeth and then headed for the small kitchen. He looked at his watch and turned the coffeepot on, filling the water container for two cups. He needed his morning coffee and he knew he was addicted to the damn stuff, but he tried to limit himself to the two cups in the morning. While waiting for the coffee to perk he walked to the small table in the middle of the living room, picking up yesterday's mail. Sitting on one of Barbara's latest acquisitions, a narrow uncomfortable chair with metal tubes everywhere, he started reading. Ripping open a letter he read the contents, making a ball of it when he was finished and tossing it toward the trashcan. He cleared all of the mail until the last envelope left was the letter from the Pentagon. He looked at it again and an odd feeling came over him, his stomach churning. He dropped the letter on the table, walked to the kitchen and filled a mug with steaming coffee. He smelled the pleasant aroma while he poured the strong Colombian and then took a sip, his eyes closed. He exhaled audibly and slowly he returned to the living room, sitting on the uncomfortable chair, picking up the letter again.

It was then that he realized the letter was addressed to Craig Beck and he raised an eyebrow in consternation. "Damn people," he muttered, taking another sip of his coffee, "they can't even get my last name right." He looked again noticing that the right address and box number were on the envelope and finally ripped it open. And his world turned upside down.

The Office of the Secretary of Defense  
The Pentagon  
Washington, D.C.

April 23, 1973  
Mr. Craig Beck  
735 Tremont Street  
Boston, Massachusetts  
Subject: Posthumous Award of the Medal of Honor (2nd Award)  
     15 May 1973, 0900 hours  
        Arlington Cemetery

Dear Mr. Beck:

The President of the United States requests the honor of your presence during the presentation of the Medal of Honor ceremony dedicated to Colonel Andrew Beck, 0416416, U.S. Army, 5th Special Forces Group, Ft. Bragg, N.C. This private ceremony will take place on May 15, 1973, 0900 hours at Arlington Cemetery. As the sole survivor of Colonel Andrew Beck, your presence is hereby requested at your father's award ceremony.

If you have any questions or for further details, please contact MSgt. Paul J. Ragsdale, at (919) 581-1990, Ft. Bragg, N.C., liaison officer for the ceremony.

Sincerely,

Elliott L. Richardson
Secretary of Defense

To say that young Craig Barlow was at a loss was an understatement. He read the letter again slowly, concentrating on the word 'father' and then he got up, the coffee cup in his hand forgotten, his mind a jumble of thoughts.

"What in the hell is going on," he mumbled aloud, dropping the letter like it was burning his fingers. He paced the floor, running his fingers through his hair, a characteristic gesture when he was upset. Forgotten was his morning run and everything else. Now he stood still, his mind mulling over the information. One more time he picked up the letter and read it, absorbing the contents slowly, noticing the word 'father' again.

This must be a joke, he thought, or someone doesn't know what the hell he is talking about. His father, Oliver Barlow, was at this very minute in bed in his house, very much alive.

So, who the hell was this Colonel Andrew Beck? And why do they think he is my father? His mind kept asking the same questions over and over again until he thought his head would split open. He looked at his watch, noticing the time, 7:00 o'clock. Where had the time gone, he thought, walking toward the bedroom. Silently he went in, walked to the closet and picked up a pair of faded jeans. He put them on quietly and then picked up a T-shirt and put that on too. Walking to the door he stopped and turned around, looking at Barbara still sleeping. For a second he thought about waking her, but then he would have to explain the letter to her and right now he didn't know what was going on. He exited the room, closing the door softly behind him. He walked fast now, reaching the coffee table and picking up the letter. With a determined look on his face he walked out. He would go and see his father about this and maybe get some answers to the whole damn puzzle. And may the lord have mercy if some stupid fool was playing a cruel joke on him.

# 3

Brookline, Boston
7 May 1973

    Craig Barlow drove fast, much too fast, but this morning he was lucky the traffic was almost non-existent at this early hour. His mind was not on his driving, his thoughts going over and over the contents of the letter. He had a hollow feeling in the pit of his stomach and somehow he knew that the letter would change his life forever. He reached the road leading to the house, driving the mile and a half up the driveway in a haze. The house was imposing; a three-story building that had been in the family for over a hundred years. It was nestled in a group of stately oaks and maples, on 47 acres of land. Through the years a room had been added here and there making the rambling house a nice, comfortable place in which to live and entertain. All the Weatherly family had lived there at one time or another and when his mother and father were married they had come to live there too. Craig had lived there most of his life, with the exception of when he was away at school and now, but the rest of the family were still there. Grandpa and grandma Weatherly had the third floor and Uncle Henry, who had never married, had the second. The rest of the house was given to Craig's parents, until his mother died. Of late, he had overheard his father talking about moving out, but so far talk was all it was. There was also a multitude of servants and a grounds keeper, all lived on the property in servant's quarters behind the house.

He reached the entrance to the house, parked his car and walked rapidly toward the door. He was reaching for the doorknob when the door opened, and a tall black man stood to the side.

"Good morning, Mister Craig," he said, smiling widely, revealing a set of incredibly white teeth. The man was 73 years old, but you couldn't tell by looking at him. He had been with the Weatherly family all his life and he and his wife had taken care of Craig Barlow when he was a child.

"Good morning, Benjamin," Craig said, walking in and smiling at the word 'mister'. Benjamin had called him that since he was a mere child learning to walk. Craig had attempted to get him to stop, but Benjamin had only smiled and continued calling him 'mister'.

"Is my father up yet?" he asked.

"Yes, Mister Craig," he answered, closing the door softly behind him. "He is in the study having breakfast and reading the newspapers."

"I'll be there with him, Benjamin," he said, walking toward the study. "Bring some coffee, please."

"Yes sir," Benjamin said. Wondering why young Craig looked so upset, he headed for the kitchen.

Craig knocked softly on the door and immediately opened it and walked in. His father was sitting behind an incredibly large and beautiful cherry desk still dressed in his silk pajamas and bathrobe, eating his breakfast and reading the newspapers. The smell of bacon and eggs was in the air and for a second, Craig's mouth watered thinking about food. The study was spacious, the walls covered by cherry paneling, lined with books from floor to ceiling, a bank of phones to one side and a computer and fax machine on another. It was simply furnished with a sofa and several chairs, all in black leather adding character to the study and a flavor that was completely masculine. Behind the immense desk, French doors flanked a stone fireplace right and left, the doors opened to a small stone walkway leading into the garden. At this time the overhead lights were on as well as a small desk lamp, which bathed the study in a soft amber light.

Oliver Barlow was an early riser, usually reading five or more newspapers before eating and today was no different, the stack of newspapers on the floor giving ample evidence to that.

He was a man of medium height, slightly overweight, his head completely bald. His eyes were as blue as the cloudless sky and framed by a face that was round and pallid with a weak chin and thin lips. What his mother had seen in Oliver Barlow was beyond Craig's imagination and he was thankful that he had inherited most of his features from the Weatherly side of the family.

"Morning, Dad", he said entering the room and walking toward the desk. They had never been close, not like a father and son, Craig thought now, his mind running amuck with all kinds of crazy thoughts. As far as he could remember, Oliver Barlow had been distant, hardly ever showing affection toward him. When he got old enough to realize those things his mother had defended his father, always excusing him as working hard or preoccupied with the business. Maybe it was because he is not really my father, Craig thought, regretting the idea as soon as he thought it. Damn, I need to stop this nonsense he told himself, stopping in front of the desk.

"Well, good morning, son," Oliver Barlow said, raising his head from the newspaper he had been reading. "What brings you over here this early in the morning?"

Craig didn't answer immediately; instead he reached for the letter in his back pocket.

"Read this," he said, handing the letter over to his father. "And then, tell me what is going on."

Oliver Barlow took the letter and then he reached for his glasses, adjusting them on his nose. For the next few seconds he was immersed in reading and then, exhaling deeply he looked at his son standing in front of the desk. He was about to say something when there was a slight knock on the door and Benjamin came in carrying a silver tray loaded with coffee and pastries. Craig and Oliver Barlow remained silent while Benjamin brought the tray in and set it on the small coffee table.

"Will there be anything else, Mister Craig?" he asked.

"No, Benjamin, that will be all, thanks," Craig said smiling at the old butler. Benjamin nodded his head and silently exited the study.

Once they were alone Craig looked at his father expectantly. "Well?" he asked, raising an eyebrow.

Oliver Barlow cleared his throat and then fixed his blue eyes on Craig. "I was hoping to talk to you about this one day, Craig," he said, getting up from the chair and coming around the desk, his expression sad. "I've been waiting for the appropriate moment ever since your mother died, but...." He stopped, looking at Craig closely, waiting for a reaction from the young man, the letter dangling from his hand, the breakfast on the desk forgotten.

"What the hell are you telling me, Dad?" he asked, his face etched in conflicting emotions. "That there is truth to this, this crap," he said, his hand pointing at the letter.

"Yes, Craig, there is," Oliver Barlow said, finality in his voice. "You better sit down and I will tell you what I can."

"Oh, Lord," Craig mumbled, his mind reeling at the import of those words. Slowly he walked to a chair, falling down in the seat like he was a lump of clay. His world was coming apart at the seams and he was not prepared for it. Nothing in his young life could have prepared him for what he was about to face and his mind rebelled at what he knew was coming.

Oliver Barlow sat opposite Craig, his hands turning the letter over and over in a nervous gesture. "I must tell you first that I loved your mother dearly and that I tried to love you as my son." He stopped talking and cleared his throat, composing himself. "But you are not my biological son," he continued. "When I married Catherine she was already pregnant with you. I had been your mother's suitor for a long time, but she didn't want anything to do with me romantically, just friends." He paused briefly, a small smile flickering across his face, remembering the early days. "Then one day your grandfather, Robert Weatherly, III, came to me with an incredible proposition. He was irate with your mother, rambling about her conduct while away from home and then he asked me if I would be interested in marrying Catherine and coming to work for the firm. He had arranged the whole thing he said, and Catherine was willing to marry me. All I had to do was give the child my name and I would be a new partner in the family business. It was much later that I found out that your grandfather had bullied, schemed and threatened her to the point that she was willing to do what he wanted and that was to marry someone of her class and to forget the redneck from Texas." He stopped again, got up from the sofa and paced the study. Craig just sat there, his mind absorbing what the man he had always thought of as his father was telling him. Part of him wanted to know all the details while another wanted to shut the words out, to close his ears to the facts he was getting.

"This was the 1950's," Oliver Barlow continued, "and in those days girls didn't tell their fathers no, especially a man like Robert Weatherly. He controlled the purse strings and the lives of all the people around him and he did it with an iron fist. He didn't want his only daughter having anything to do with a penniless cowboy from Texas and he saw me as his way out. I was in love with your mother, Craig. I was young and the lure of coming to work for Weatherly and Son, as the company was called in those days, was a heady experience. I said yes and when you were born my name was put on the birth certificate as your father."

He stopped pacing and came to stand by Craig, their eyes locked on each other.

"The old man swore me to secrecy and forbade your mother to ever talk to anyone about this. She went to her grave with her secret, son, but I know that she didn't want you to find out about your real father like this, from a letter. I always thought that one day she would have been the one to tell you the whole story." He folded the letter carefully and handed it to Craig.

"There is not much more I can tell you about your real father, Craig," he said, his voice soft, almost a murmur. "I never met the man and your mother never talked about him either, so I can't reveal any details about him."

He walked to the desk and sat down heavily on the leather chair, his brow creased in thought.

"I don't know how far you want to pursue this, son, but if you want to know the whole story then you better talk with your Uncle Henry. He was there from the beginning and he knew your father."

At those words, Craig's head came up sharply, his eyes fastened on the man who until a few moments ago he had always thought of as his 'father'.

"Are you telling me that Uncle Henry knows this man who is supposed to be my father?" he asked, his voice full of sarcasm. "You know, this gets better and better all the time." He stopped, his face now full of annoyance.

"I wish I could make this easier on you, Craig," Oliver Barlow said, his voice now tired and sad, a look of resignation on his face. "But you have to find your own way with this."

He got up from the chair and made his way slowly toward the door. He stopped in front of Craig, his hand reaching out to touch the young man on the shoulder. For a moment his hand lingered there and then, with a final squeeze he dropped his hand and was gone, leaving Craig alone with his thoughts.

He sat still for a long time, his mind mulling over the conversation that had transpired between he and his father a few moments ago. Finally he got up and walked out of the study. Once outside he looked around for Benjamin, finding him in the kitchen with his wife, Carlotta. She was busy cleaning breakfast dishes and he approached her from behind, hugging her tightly and planting a kiss on her cheek.

"How is my favorite nanny?" he asked, letting her go.

Carlotta laughed and turned around to look at him. "I'm fine child," she said, her eyes looking the young man up and down, "but you look like you haven't had a decent meal in ages. Now sit down and I'll fix you breakfast."

"I'm sorry, Carlotta, but I'm not hungry," Craig said.

Carlotta took a step toward him and looked him straight in the eye. She was an imposing woman, almost three hundred pounds of love and affection, but when she was mad at you and she looked at you the way she was looking at Craig right now, he knew better than to argue with her.

Seeing the look on her face he graciously capitulated. "Okay, okay. I'll eat something." He didn't feel like eating at all, his stomach was all tied up in knots, but he needed time to think. He was at a loss about what to do next. Did he really want to know more or would it be better just to let it go and forget about the whole thing? The man was dead anyway, so what good would it do anyone to find out who he was?

"That's much better," she said, swinging her ponderous figure back to the stove. "I'll fix your favorites, pancakes and sausages."

Craig heard a small laugh behind him and he turned to see Benjamin smiling widely at him. "There is no arguing with that woman, son," he said, coming to stand next to him. The kitchen was immense with all the modern conveniences. To one side there was a small nook with a table and chairs and Craig and Benjamin sat down waiting for the food. Carlotta came by with a pot of coffee, set two cups in front of them and went back to her cooking, leaving the men alone.

They sipped the strong brew silently for a few seconds and then Benjamin looked at Craig. Something was bothering the young man, something that had him preoccupied and morose. The food came and while old Benjamin ate with gusto, Craig barely touched his.

You know, Mister Craig," he started talking, his voice soft, almost a whisper, "I have known you since you were a pain in your mamma's stomach and when you were born, me and Carlotta took care of you until you were old enough to go to school." He paused for a second, sipping his coffee. Craig stopped eating and was looking at his old friend intently.

"I'm an old man now and life has given me much to be thankful for. Your family, especially your mother and your Uncle Henry, have been more than generous to us and we have had a good life here." He stopped again, his eyes fixed on Craig's face.

"We never had children of our own and for us you were a blessing. We loved you like you were a part of us and if there is ever anything that we can do for you I would be proud to help you, son."

Craig Barlow heard the words and a lump came to his throat. He reached over the table, his hand closing on Benjamin's arm.

"Thank you," he said simply, his eyes shining with unshed tears. In a split second he made up his mind and the words came out in a torrent. He told Benjamin everything, even about the talk with his father and when he finished he was spent, like he had run a hundred miles. Through it all, Carlotta left them alone, casting a glance in their direction every once in a while, but otherwise leaving them to themselves. Through all this Benjamin sat still, hardly blinking his eyes, listening to the young man.

"So there it is, Benjamin," he said, "this morning I was Craig Barlow and now I don't know who I really am or what I want to do with this information." He was quiet for a moment trying to find the right words to express his feelings. "It's like part of me wants to know this man, what part of me is like him, and then…I don't know," he said, throwing his hands in the air.

Benjamin cleared his throat and looked around, making sure they were alone. "I must tell you son that I have known about this since you were born," he said softly, his eyes locked on Craig's. Seeing the look on Craig's face he continued. "Your mother confided in Carlotta about her young handsome soldier and about her pregnancy and we were happy for her. But then everything turned ugly when your grandfather made her marry a man she didn't love." He sipped some more of the lukewarm coffee, his old eyes now misty with memories. "Talk to your Uncle Henry son, he can help you a lot with your feelings."

Craig sighed deeply, nodding his head. He drained his coffee cup and got up.

"I think I'll do that," he said. "Where is Uncle Henry now?"

"He left early this morning for the office, son. You know it's Saturday and he always works on Saturdays.

"Thank you, Benjamin," Craig said, clasping the old man to his chest, letting go and heading for the door.

Old Benjamin saw him go and shook his head. What had started over twenty years ago was coming back to haunt them again. And when old man Weatherly found out what was going on, the shit would really hit the fan, Benjamin thought, shaking his head and walking to his wife's side. Embracing her tenderly he spoke softly to her and when he had finished he saw tears rolling down her wrinkled cheeks, a sad look etched on her face.

# 4

Weatherly, Weatherly & Barlow
Cambridge Street
Boston MA
7 May 1973

 Henry Weatherly was sitting at his desk going over some contracts when his secretary knocked discretely on the door and then walked in. Mary Jo Weinmann had been employed by the firm all her adult life and had been Henry's executive secretary for the last ten years. She was efficient and personable and as far as Henry Weatherly was concerned—indispensable. She came in and stopped at the desk, her hands clasped together in a characteristic gesture when she was concerned about something. She was a fifty-two year old widow and didn't mind working half days on Saturdays or going on business trips all over the country with Mr. Weatherly. That and the not so humble salary that Henry Weatherly paid her made everything satisfactory for her. Besides that, she really enjoyed working for Henry Weatherly, deriving enormous satisfaction from being 'almost indispensable' to him as Mr. Weatherly put it.

"Yes?" Henry Weatherly asked, seeing the look on her face.

"Young Craig is outside, Mr. Weatherly," she said, "and he is extremely upset about something. He wants to talk to you."

"Well, by all means Mary Jo," he said politely, a smile flickering across his face, "send him in."

"Yes sir," she said, walking out of the office.

Henry Weatherly got up slowly, stretching his right leg. The damn thing was always giving him pain, even when he was sitting down. He was a tall man with a slight build, almost skinny for his frame. He was immaculately dressed in a three-piece gray suit, even on Saturday when nobody would be coming by the office. He was a stickler for formalities and if you were going to the office to work, then by God you better dress appropriately. His eyes were the color of burnt almonds, large and intelligent. His hair was a light brown, meticulously combed, speckled with silver strands here and there, his hairline receding. In the business circle that he frequented he was known as a brilliant businessman and ever since he had become the chairman of the firm, the balance sheet had grown tremendously to the delight of the shareholders. He came around the desk facing the door, waiting for his nephew to walk in, wondering what had gone wrong in Craig's life that he needed to see him on Saturday morning.

Craig walked in and saw his uncle standing by the desk. The office was large and impressive. Henry Weatherly believed the clients had to be comfortable and if possible in a certain awe of their surroundings. There was no need to pretend that the firm was not rich, as long as it was done in style and with taste. The furniture was elegant and comfortable and the artwork on the paneled walls was the real thing, not reproduction.

As Craig entered his eyes drifted to the plaque behind Uncle Henry's chair. The plaque was in contrast to the rest of the office but as far as Craig could tell it had always been there. He remembered the first time he really saw it he was still a young boy and he had asked his uncle about the shiny medals, wanting to touch them and play with them. His uncle had let him know real fast that those medals were not toys and not to play with them. Much later, when he was a lot older and wiser he had found out the truth and the reason for the plaque to be behind the desk and how important it was for Uncle Henry. He had read the caption below the medals and had marveled at the words, wondering if Uncle Henry was not a warrior in disguise. There were three things on the plaque and his uncle had spent a lot of time explaining to him what they were and what they represented. The first one he had learned was a Combat Infantryman's Badge and the other two were medals. One medal was shaped in the form of a star and he had found out that it was a Silver Star, the other shaped in the form of a heart with the image of President George Washington engraved on it was purple, therefore the name, the Purple Heart. They were army medals and his uncle had finally told him the story behind them. It seems that Uncle Henry had enlisted in the Army during the Korean conflict, and become some sort of signal officer and assigned to the rear echelon in some obscure post that no one thought was anywhere near the front lines. He had wanted a commission as a finance officer, but the Army, in its infinite wisdom, had decided that he would be better off as a signal officer so there he was. There were no predetermined front or rear lines and one night without warning the whole battalion found itself engaged in a fight for its life. North Koreans swarmed all over the place in a pre-dawn attack. To the sound of mortars and small arms weapons, cooks, bakers, signalmen, enlisted men, officers and everybody else who could handle a weapon was rushed to the lines to stem the red avalanche. After the battle was over the company commander had recommended Uncle Henry for the two medals, the Silver Star and Purple Heart. The caption read:

Headquarters
Department of the Army

Award of the Silver Star
5 December 1950

By order of the President of the United States the Silver Star is hereby awarded to 1st Lieutenant Henry Weatherly, 0 9132476, Signal Corp., United States Army.

Citation: For a period of two days, November 26-27, 1950, then 2nd Lieutenant Henry Weatherly was engaged in military operations against hostile forces in the area of Sesim-ni, Republic of Korea. Lt. Weatherly distinguished himself when at approximately 0200 hours his company came under weathering enemy fire. Showing tremendous courage after his company commander was wounded; Lt. Weatherly assumed command of the company and rallied his men to attack the superior enemy forces streaming down toward them. Rushing the incoming enemy, Lt. Weatherly emptied his carbine, killing a score of the enemy while at the same time suffering a wound to his right leg. Refusing medical help and ignoring his wound, he continued the attack, throwing grenades at the enemy and urging his men to fight. Charging the enemy with indomitable courage and with complete disregard for his life, Lt. Weatherly closed with them in hand-to-hand combat, inspiring his men to charge the enemy and halt their advance. His sustained courage and fighting spirit against incredible odds reflect the utmost glory upon himself and the traditions of the United States Army.

There was another caption next to the one about the Silver Star with similar wording concerning the Purple Heart and the wounds that Uncle Henry had received during the fight.

Uncle Henry was extremely proud of the plaque and well he should be, Craig thought, coming to stand beside his uncle. The look on Craig's face was a telltale sign that something was very wrong and Henry Weatherly looked at him with concern in his eyes. The boy was upset, Henry thought, no doubt about it.

He leveled his gaze at his nephew and waited, wondering what was coming. "Uncle Henry, I need to talk with you," Craig said, his voice almost trembling. Damn, but he is all shook up about something, Henry Weatherly thought, catching the trembling in his nephew's voice.

"Sit down, Craig, please," he said, himself walking around to his desk and sitting down. "Tell me what has happened to get you in this shape?" He had never seen Craig Barlow in such a state before and his heart jumped thinking that something terrible had happened at home.

"I want you to read this letter and then talk to me." He handed the letter to his uncle and then continued. "I must tell you that I've talked to my father and Benjamin and they have told me some of the facts about this, but I'm not satisfied. I want to know more."

He said that with finality, like he had just made up his mind, Henry thought, beginning to unfold the letter.

He read slowly, finishing the letter in a few seconds, his face expressionless. Putting the letter down he got up and ran a hand over his face, a pained expression etched on it.

"So he is dead," he said, and Craig realized that it was a statement, not a question.

"Yes, Uncle Henry," Craig said, inching forward in his chair. "Whoever this Colonel Andrew Beck is or was is dead, according to that letter."

"He was your father," Henry Weatherly said, a hard edge to his voice now. "Just like that letter said. He was a man of honor and a friend."

"My father?" Craig said sarcastically now, getting up from the chair and jamming his hands in his pockets. "Well, it would have been nice if someone had decided to tell me that I had another "daddy" somewhere, before the man died." He was mad now, his stomach churning, his mind a jumble of thoughts.

"I understand your feelings, son," Henry said softly. "But I always thought that the responsibility to tell you about Andrew Beck was your mother's, not mine or Oliver's."

"But instead, I have to find out that another man is my real father by a letter from the Pentagon," Craig said, his voice rough with emotion. Then controlling his mounting anger he sat down again. Getting mad was not going to solve anything. He was quiet for a moment, gathering his thoughts. He massaged his face with both hands, finally looking at Uncle Henry again.

"What happened, Uncle Henry?" he asked, his tone now neutral. "Benjamin said that you knew all of it."

"Andrew Beck was your father, but he never knew he had a son until several months ago when I told him," Henry Weatherly said. "You see, Andrew Beck was a career officer in the Army and it took me a while to find him. When I did find him for the first time I tried hard to get your mother to let him know that he had a son, but she would never agree to do that, going so far as to make me promise her that I would not do it either. I really don't know why she didn't want me to say anything or why she was so obstinate about him not knowing about you. I guess she thought it would interfere with his life in some way, or that he would reject you." He stopped for a second, his mind trying to gather the old facts together. "She really didn't have to worry about Andrew rejecting you," he continued, "He was a man of honor and most of all he loved your mother. I also found out that he had won the Medal of Honor in Korea, the highest honor that a soldier can obtain from a grateful nation, Craig, and that he had acted with great courage and bravery in the face of overwhelming odds." Henry walked back to the desk, lowering himself to the chair, his hands massaging his temple. This talking about the past was something that made him tired, his mind refusing to accept the fact that Andrew Beck was dead. He had really only known the man for about two weeks, but the young man had left a lasting impression on him. He looked at Craig, who was in turn watching him expectantly, waiting for him to continue. Henry Weatherly smiled a tired smile and started talking again.

"It was late 1950 and I had joined the Army, much to the chagrin of my father. I had become an officer and had gone to Columbus, GA in order to take care of some business for the firm before shipping for Korea. While I was there your mother and some of our cousins decided to come and pay a visit and ended up staying for two weeks. The girls had this crazy notion that they could help the war effort by working at the local USO club, and they volunteered their efforts. It was while in Columbus that I met Andrew Beck, a fortuitous occasion for me since he probably saved my life and…" Henry Weatherly cut himself off, clearing his throat. His eyes were bright and shiny and for a second Craig thought his uncle would cry. But he didn't. Looking at the clock on the wall he got up and went to a cabinet on the far wall of the office. Opening the bottom door he came out with a bottle of Canadian Mist and soda water. He was not a drinker and it was too damn early in the morning, but at an occasion like this a stiff drink didn't sound like a bad idea. He fixed himself a stiff one, taking small cubes of ice from a glass decanter, filling the glass mostly with the dark amber liquid and then raising his eyebrows to Craig, in a silent question. Craig shook his head no, and Henry came back to the desk, sipping his drink. He met Craig's eyes again and the story continued.

"I was walking in downtown Columbus fairly late one night when I made the mistake of walking through an alley. Three drunken GI's jumped me and were in the process of kicking the daylights out of me when another man intervened, rousting the drunkards with some hard punches." He paused momentarily, a smile flickering across his face as he remembered the fight. "It was your father, Andrew, and needless to say I was happy that he had come to my aid. He was a private then and was on leave just before shipping for Korea also. I was filthy and bleeding and he decided to go with me to the USO Club to look for my sister. The moment I introduced him to Catherine it was all over. From there on they didn't have eyes for anyone else. Your mother was a beautiful woman, Craig, kind of shy, petite, almost fragile and she hit it off with the tall Texas cowboy immediately. He was in town for two weeks and then he was off to Korea. He and your mother became inseparable and I was happy for her. At the same time I was worried, knowing our father would not approve of a penniless cowboy and his only daughter. And I was right. When it came time for Andrew and me to go to Korea, Catherine went back to Boston. It was much later, through Carlotta that I learned she was pregnant. Our father went through the roof, wanting her to abort the child, coming down hard on her." Henry stopped talking, pain and sadness etched on his weathered face. He hadn't been present when his sister had gone through the bad times with their father, but he knew that it had been bad. He knew his father and the old man's ways and he was certain that Catherine had gone through hell before she was forced to marry Oliver. When he had returned from Korea, Catherine was a broken woman and he had felt utter contempt for his father. He had tried to raise the subject of Andrew Beck with his sister but it was like a taboo subject, his sister refused to discuss it.

Craig Barlow sat in his chair, his hands clasped together, listening intently to his uncle, not missing a word.

"I kept my promise to her until she died," he continued, "then I found your father again and told him about you, asked him to come here to Boston and he did. This was about the time of your special ceremony concerning the athletic awards, several months ago. He was devastated at first knowing that he had a son he had never seen or shared his life with. He was on his way to Vietnam for the second or third time and he promised that on his return he would make arrangements to see you and talk with you. He wanted to spend time with you, wanted to try and build some kind of relationship with the only person that was left of his blood. But he never made it back," Henry Weatherly said, a tone of finality in his voice, his eyes drifting to the letter lying on top of the desk.

There was silence in the office for a long time, until Henry Weatherly broke it again. He glanced at his nephew and forged ahead.

"At least he was able to meet you, if only briefly."

At that Craig's head came up sharply, his eyes now locked on his uncle's face. "What did you say, Uncle Henry?" he asked, his face showing the surprise that the statement had produced.

"Yes, son," he said, "at your ceremony at Harvard, about six months ago. He was there, very briefly, but there nonetheless."

"I don't understand, Uncle Henry," Craig Barlow said. "You mean that I have met my…my father?" He stumbled over the word, thinking that he was betraying the man he thought all his life was his real father, Oliver Barlow. It was hard for him to think of the man that they were talking about as his father, his mind refusing to acknowledge the fact just yet.

"Yes, like I said, on the day of your athletic ceremony at Harvard," Henry Weatherly answered. "I was talking to a man in uniform when you came over. You were introduced and shortly afterwards the man left. Remember?"

"Oh God, yes, I remember," Craig said, his mind reaching for the elusive moment, bringing it back in focus. He had seen his uncle standing close to the exit of the auditorium, a tall man in uniform standing by his side. At that moment he had thought that the man was just another one of the hundreds of visitors that had come to the ceremony, just someone talking to his uncle. He had approached them and when he was close enough he had thought that the man was familiar, that he had seen him somewhere or that the man reminded him of someone he knew. The man had been dressed in officer's Class A greens, his pants bloused inside jumpboots.

He remembered the man's eyes, almost green, eyes of incredible intensity, shining with an inner glimmer. And he remembered how those eyes had lighted up with something like pride when he was introduced and how strong was the handgrip of the stranger when they shook hands. His voice had been strong, firm, with a slight southern accent. The man had exuded self-confidence, like a person who didn't have any doubts about who he was or where he was going in life and there was an aura about him that made you feel that all was well and secured. He was the eternal warrior, ever vigilant at the gate, to ensure that the country was safe. He had been impressed by the man's military bearing, ramrod straight and by the incredible number of medals on his chest. He had recognized the Combat Infantryman's Badge, one just like his Uncle Henry's, but with two stars above that he didn't know what they represented, also the Purple Heart and then he was lost. He didn't have the slightest idea what the other medals represented or what they were for, but was sure that the man standing in front of him had earned each and every one of them. They had talked briefly and then the man had looked at him straight in the eyes. Something like an indescribable sadness and longing etched deeply on his face. The gray-green eyes stayed fixed on him for a long time, making him uncomfortable and then the man's whole body shook like one possessed of a fever. But whatever it was, the man took control again, his face becoming non-committal, like a mask. He shook Craig's hand one more time and then, carefully, putting a green beret on his head, walked away. Craig was left standing next to his uncle with a feeling that something important had just happened, what he couldn't tell. He had never thought about the man again until now. Damn, but I could close my eyes and see him standing there talking, those gray-green eyes fixed on me, Craig thought running his hand through his hair. For some reason he shuddered. He got up and paced the office while his uncle watched him.

"Well, Uncle Henry, where do I go from here?" he asked, coming to stand by the desk.

"I don't know, son," Henry said, coming to stand by his nephew's side. "Every man has the right to know where he comes from, what kind of blood runs in his veins. You can stop now and forget about Andrew Beck, or you can continue on your quest to find out that your father was one of those people who made this country great. He was a man who answered the call of duty, for God and country and who gave his life for those principles."

Craig Barlow didn't answer; looking at his uncle he nodded his head and walked softly out of the office, closing the door silently behind him.

Henry Weatherly saw him go and part of his heart went with him. He knew the boy was confused and upset. To find out that your father was someone other than the person you thought was a heavy blow for anyone. He shook his head and stood leaning on the side of his desk, his brow creased in thought. Reaching a decision, Henry Weatherly punched a button on his telephone. Almost immediately Mrs. Weinmann's voice came across.

"Yes sir," she said.

"Mary Jo, get the Secretary of Defense on the line for me at the White House or at the Pentagon."

"Yes sir," she answered, clearing the line.

In a short time his telephone buzzed again and he picked it up. Saying hello, he listened to the voice of Elliot L. Richardson, Secretary of Defense for President Richard Nixon. They had been classmates in college, Elliott going into politics while he had decided on business and the family firm. Through the years they kept in touch, exchanging favors now and then.

"Elliott, I need a personal favor," he said.

"Of course, Henry, whatever you need," Richardson said, wondering what his friend wanted. "Just shoot."

He had known Henry Weatherly just about all his life and Henry had helped the Republican Party countless times with favors and money. Come election time they knew they could count on him for their fund raising and that he would bring the money in. He was also a personal friend of the President and Richardson knew that whatever it was that Henry Weatherly wanted, he would get it.

"On 15 May, there will be a ceremony at Arlington, a Medal of Honor presentation for Colonel Andrew Beck," Henry said softly, his voice even, the Boston accent precise. " I want an invitation to it."

"Andrew Beck you said?" Richardson said. "Hold on." He waited while Richardson talked to someone, probably his secretary, the muffled voices coming through the earpiece and shortly after Richardson was back on the line.

"Yes that's correct, Henry, he is scheduled for the fifteenth," he said, his mind now wondering why one of the richest men in Boston was interested in a lowly Colonel. "I'll instruct my secretary to send you an invitation and I'll personally inform the President that you are coming," he said. "I'm sure he will be delighted to see you, Henry."

"Thanks, Elliot, I owe you one."

They talked for a few more minutes promising to see each other soon and then Henry Weatherly hung up. He looked at his wristwatch, noticing the time. It was still early but he didn't feel like working anymore. Walking to his chair he sat down heavily, stretching his legs. He punched the intercom, listening to the familiar voice.

"Yes, Mr. Weatherly?" Mary Jo said.

"Let's go home, Mrs. Weinmann," he said, his voice now sounding tired, far away. He got up slowly, favoring the limp on his right leg and made his way to the door. He stopped and looked around, his mind crowded with thoughts. For a moment his eyes were fixed on the plaque behind his chair. He shook his head slowly like a man trying to get rid of some unpleasant thought and then he opened the door, exited the room and closed the door softly behind him.

# 5

Boston, MA
8 May 1973

    Craig Barlow drove aimlessly for hours after leaving his uncle's office. He was in a daze, his brain trying hard to absorb and comprehend the information that had come to him so unexpectedly. This morning he had gotten up like any other morning, a well to do young man with a bright future ahead of him, a member of one of the most prominent families in the area. And now things had changed with a speed that left him numb and out of place. In a way he was the same Craig Barlow he had always been, in another he felt like his life had taken a turn in which he had to face things he had never dreamed of. That Oliver Barlow was not his father he could understand, but the fact that his real father had been a soldier and war hero was something else. He had been opposed to the war, demonstrated against it, even if half-heartedly, and now he had to contend with a man unknown to him, a man who had given his life for a cause, for an idea, for his country. He had never met anyone like that and for him it was inconceivable that a person could go to the grave defending an idea, a principle. Something like that spoke of an incredible commitment and Craig knew that he had never really been tested. All his life he had been spoiled, never thinking about giving anything back, never dreaming that there were people out there who could face death with incredible courage and lay down their lives for others, for words like duty, freedom, and country. And now this man who was supposed to be his father had done just that and was dead. He couldn't get any answers from him to his questions, couldn't get to know him and find out what kind of man he was. The fact that Uncle Henry had liked him and respected him was something that Craig understood and that said a lot about the man, but that was not enough. If he was ever to reconcile the fact that Andrew Beck was his father then he needed to find out more. Part of him felt badly about the fact that he was trying to find out things about this man that had come into his life so unexpectedly. Oliver Barlow had been in his life since he was a baby and he thought of him as his father. This made Craig feel like he was betraying him somehow, but on the other hand he was curious, intrigued by Andrew Beck and his life, wondering what part of himself was like him. And what was he going to do after he found out what he wanted about this man? Was he going to let the whole world know that Oliver Barlow was not his real father? Change his name? And what if he found out that Andrew Beck was not the kind of person he thought he was? All those questions and more crowded in his head, clamoring to be heard, expecting an answer.

 He shook his head to clear it and found himself parked in front of his apartment. How he got there or how long he had been there he didn't know. He sat in his car with the engine running for a long time and finally snapped out of it. He turned the engine off and got out of the car slowly. He was tired mentally and physically, but he knew that there would be no sleep for him for a long time. He walked to the apartment letting himself in. The place was dark and he wondered about Barbara. It was now nighttime and he had left early in the morning while she was still in bed. He was glad she was not there. He didn't have the slightest idea what he was going to tell her. He flipped on a light and walked to the small living room and sat down heavily on the sofa. There was a note laying on the coffee table and he picked it up, reading the contents slowly. She had gone to spend the evening with friends and was mad at him for not calling or letting her know where he was. He dropped the note on the floor and leaned his head back, his eyes closed. For minutes he was still, then he reached for his back pocket and extracted the letter again. Something had been pushing to get through in his muddled brain, something to do with a name and a phone number. He smoothed the paper and read the letter again, finding what he was looking for. There had been a name in the P.S. Something about a liaison officer and a place called Ft. Bragg, North Carolina. Maybe this man has some answers for me, Craig thought, reaching for the phone and dialing the number on the paper.

A child's voice answered the phone and in the background he could hear voices and laughter. For a second he thought about hanging up but then he heard the voice again and he plunged ahead.

"Hello, hello," the child's voice said.

Craig looked at the name on the letter and hurried to answer the child. The voice was that of a very young child and he wondered if he could get her to understand what he wanted.

"I need to talk with Paul J. Ragsdale," he said, his voice sounding loud.

"Hello, hello," the small voice said again. He was about to hang up when he heard a man's voice close to his ear.

"Caroline, how many times have I told you not to play with the phone?" There were some giggles at the other end of the line and then a strong voice said, "hello."

"I need to talk to Paul J. Ragsdale," he said again, wishing he had not placed the call.

"Speaking," the voice said.

"Mr. Ragsdale, my name is…"

The strong voice cut him off suddenly. "I'm Master Sergeant Ragsdale, mister," the man said, "and what can I do for you?"

"Like I said," Craig started again, "I'm Craig Barlow and I would like to talk to you about Colonel Andrew Beck."

For a moment there was silence at the other end of the line and then the man spoke.

"Who did you say you are?"

"I'm Craig Barlow."

"I'm sorry mister, but I don't know any Craig Barlow."

"I know you don't know me, but you do know Colonel Andrew Beck?" he said, feeling like he was loosing it.

There was some hesitation at the other end of the line and then the man answered him. "Yes, I knew Andrew Beck," the man said. "He was my best friend."

"I'm his… his son." Craig said, wondering why the word gave him so much trouble.

"Oh hell, yes," the voice changing now and then like an afterthought, "the letter. You got the letter."

"Yes, I got the letter," Craig replied.

"Well I was wondering if you would have the guts to call," Ragsdale said. "But then you are Andrew's boy and I couldn't expect any less from you".

For some unknown reason , those words made Craig feel good and he smiled.

"I want to talk about him", he said, the words rushing out of his mouth. "I 've a million questions to ask and…".

Once again the voice at the other end of the line cut him off.

"If you have the time son and you really want to know about your father, come to Ft. Bragg, North Carolina. Call this number when you get in and I'll give you directions to my place". With that and without waiting for an answer, the phone went dead.

Craig sat pensively for a while and then he made his decision. What the heck, he thought, I'm not doing anything important right now and I can spare a couple of days away from here. He got up quickly, his mind made up, throwing a few things in an overnight bag, making sure he had enough money and grabbing and old Atlas. He looked for the place, Ft. Bragg and found it, next to a town named Fayetteville in North Carolina. He looked at the roads, calculating that the trip would take him close to ten hours. He thought about Barbara again, knowing that she would be royally piss at him and he shrugged his shoulders. He had to know the answers to his questions and this was important to him, so she was going to have to accept it. Hurriedly, he scribble a note for her, telling her that he had gone to North Carolina to take care of some personal business. He dropped the note on the coffee table and with a last look around the place he exited the apartment.

He drove above the speed limit for most of the night, fighting to keep his eyes open. For a while traffic was light in the interstate, eventually getting worse until it was bumper to bumper. Finally, after driving two hundred miles and unable to keep from falling sleep at the wheel any longer, he stopped at a fleabag motel. He was hungry and tired and after getting a room, he walked across the street to a hamburger joint that was opened all night. After that he slept and was back on the road after just three hours, his mind to restless to let him sleep any longer. He was still tired, his eyes feeling like he had sandpaper in them, but after several miles he started to feel better. He drove into the night, the miles passing swiftly, something inside of him telling him that he was on a journey that would change his life irrevocably.

The first hint of daylight was showing in the sky when Craig saw the sign—Fayetteville 57 miles. Well, he thought, I'll be in this Ft. Bragg within the hour. He drove the rest of the way without any trouble and by the time the sun was warming the morning, Craig Barlow arrive at Ft. Bragg. He fell in behind a line of cars and his eyes drifted to the sign at the entrance. In big block letters the sign proclaimed that this was Ft.

Bragg, home of the 82nd Airborne Division, "the All American" and XVIII ABN. Corps.

He was stopped at the main gate by a young man with an armband on his right arm, the letters M.P. emblazoned on it, a pistol holstered at his side. The young soldier looked at the car and approached him asking for his business. After Craig explained that he was on personal business, the young man handed him a visitor's pass and a map of the military reservation. He drove aimlessly for a while, just looking, absorbing the sights. He had never seen a military post in his life and was amazed at the size of this particular one. There were people and cars everywhere, new and old buildings, soldiers in uniform, and every once in a while, he could see helicopters flying in the distance. He finally stopped at a pay phone at a hamburger joint, dialed the number from the letter again and waited to hear the same voice. This time the voice was female, pleasant and warm, saying hello.

"Yes," Craig said, wondering who the woman was. "I'm Craig Barlow and I need…" He was interrupted in mid sentence, the voice at the other end of the line sounding a little surprised.

"Well, I'm glad you made it," the woman said. "I bet Paul that you would be here before the day was over." And then, without waiting for an answer, he heard her yelling for someone.

"Paul…Paul, come to the phone," she yelled, without bothering to cover the mouthpiece, making Craig jump at the shrill sound assaulting his ear. And then again, "Andrew's boy is here."

"Jesus!" Craig said, jerking the phone off his ear and shaking his head to clear it. Tentatively he placed the phone back, waiting for more yelling, but the seconds passed and the line was silent. He waited, felling like a fool. I'm so predictable that they knew I was coming?" he thought. He was jolted out of his reverie by the same strong voice that he had heard before. There was no hello, no nothing, just straight to the point.

"Where are you?" Master Sergeant Paul J. Ragsdale said.

"I'm at some hamburger joint in the middle of this place," Craig said. Something with the name of "Harris Burger joint."

"Yeah, well stay put," the man said, "you are just minutes from where I live," and he hung up.

Craig Barlow looked at the phone in his hand like something alien and then put it down, shaking his head again. He walked out of the joint and sat down in his car, wondering how long he would have to wait before this Paul J. Ragsdale would show up. Once again the thoughts started running wild in his head, wondering what he really was doing in this place. The military was something that he didn't know anything about, had never been involved with, and here he was now, in the middle of some God-forsaken military reservation looking for answers to his life. But his 'father' apparently had been very successful at it, making a career of the military and attaining some measure of success. Hell, the man was a war hero, not just once but twice, if the award he was about to receive was any indication of a man's worth within the military. At least his Uncle Henry thought it was, Craig remembered, shaking his head to clear it. If Mr. Ragsdale doesn't show up soon, he thought, I'll be sound asleep shortly. He stifled a yawn and looked around, his mind going back again to the words that his uncle had uttered one day about the medal. According to him, the Medal of Honor was the highest honor the nation could bestow on their warriors, epitomizing the principles that made this nation great; honor, God, country, and devotion to duty. It was not something that was given lightly, and a man had to act with complete disregard for his life, above and beyond the call of duty, in order to receive it. He remembered other words like conspicuous gallantry, intrepidity, high words to live by and according to Uncle Henry, words that very few men were able to adhere to.

He fell asleep in the car until a hand woke him by shaking his shoulder roughly. He came awake with a start, sat straight up in the car, looking around wildly. For a moment panic assailed him, becoming disoriented, his mind refusing to tell him where he was. He looked out of the left window to find a man staring at him, a smile etched on his face. He was a tall, fair skinned man, massively built with short blond hair. The man looked to be in his early thirties, but was in fact almost forty-four years old. He had a weathered face and laughing blue eyes that could freeze a person's soul when mad. He was dressed in civilian clothes, blue jeans and a black T-shirt with brown loafers on his feet. The man looked tanned and healthy, just like a soldier, Craig thought, wondering if his father had looked anything like this man. He knew before the man spoke that he was looking at Master Sgt. Paul J. Ragsdale. He exited the car and faced the man.

"You must be Craig," the man said, a warm smile on his face. "Andrew's boy."

"I'm Craig Barlow," he responded, annoyance in his voice.

"Well, that's fine," Paul Ragsdale answered, laughter in his voice now, "but to me you are Andrew's boy." He extended his hand toward Craig. Their eyes fixed on each other.

Craig didn't answer, taking a step forward and grasping the man's hand. The handshake was strong, firm, and Ragsdale thought that the boy shook hands just like his father.

"You know," he said, a trace of sadness in his voice, "you look just like him, the same height, the same eyes, even the way your face pout and your expressions." They looked at each other for long seconds and then Craig smiled, breaking the ice.

"Your father was my best friend, more like a brother," he said. "We were together for over twenty years, all over the world." He paused for a second, the memories surging to the surface again. It was hard to believe that Andrew was dead, and now looking at this young man in front of him; it was more like a ghost had come to visit. He took a step back, his eyes shining bright. He shook his head and forced a smile on his face, changing the subject.

"Nice car you have here," he said, his eyes taking in the beautiful lines of the black 69 Corvette in front of him.

"Thanks," Craig said, his eyes going to his car. It was filthy with road grime, but the car was still impressive. He looked up again to see Ragsdale leaning against a red, 69 Corvette, a smile on his face. They broke into a laugh at the coincidence of both having the same car, just different colors.

"Let's go home," Ragsdale said. "Just follow me."

"Okay," Craig called back, getting into his car, shifting gears and following the red Corvette out of the parking lot. In a few minutes they pulled into a housing section and Craig noticed that all the houses were built just alike. In front of each house there was a sign giving the name and rank of the inhabitant. They stopped at one of the houses the sign proclaiming that Master Sgt. Paul J. Ragsdale was the occupant at this time. Craig didn't have any idea what a Master Sgt. was and he realized how ignorant he was about military matters. I'm going to have to learn something about all this he thought, parking his car behind the other. He grabbed his bag and followed Ragsdale up a narrow sidewalk behind the building. A small deck had been built next to the rear entrance and they walked through it entering the house by the kitchen. It was a small unit, simply furnished. Besides the kitchen/dining room, there was a living room, a desk on a corner serving as a study. To the right a hallway led to a bathroom and two bedrooms. A small gas fireplace could be seen in another corner, a wooden mantle over it, holding numerous pictures. Pictures of children and a woman could be seen in some of them and Paul J. Ragsdale could be seen in others, sometimes with the woman and in others with several soldiers around him. In one particular picture there were two men, their arms around each other's shoulders, a smile etched on their faces. They were about the same height, one was Ragsdale and the other, Craig would swear, was the man he had met at the graduation ceremony, his 'father'. He took a step toward the picture and was brought out of his reverie by Ragsdale's voice.

"This is home sweet home," Ragsdale said, a hint of irony in his voice. "The Army is not known for luxurious apartments as you can see."

Craig looked around, nodding his head. The place was small and cramped and he wondered how the whole family could live here. He knew that there were children in the house or at least a child and also a wife or whoever that was on the phone last time he called. And then, Ragsdale cleared that up in his next statement.

"The wife and children are at church, so we are by ourselves until they return," Ragsdale said. "You get the children's room for as long as you want to stay."

"There is no need for that Paul," Craig said. "I can get a motel room for a few days and not put the children out."

"Nonsense," Paul said, a smile flickering across his rugged features, "the little devils would love to stay in bed with us anyway."

Craig sat down his bag, stifling a yawn. Damn, but he was tired.

"Would you like a drink or soda?" Ragsdale asked, looking at him.

"No thanks," Craig answered. "What I would really like to do is to lay down for a couple of hours. I'm bushed."

"No problem," Ragsdale said, noticing the weariness in the young man's eyes. "First room on the right. Just go in and make yourself at home. I'll wake you up in a couple of hours and then we will talk."

Craig didn't answer, just nodded his head. Picking up his bag he walked to the bedroom, opened the door and entered. The room was small with bunk beds to one side. Children's toys and clothes were scattered everywhere and the beds were unmade. Barbara would have a fit at something like this, he thought, pushing the toys and clothes aside from one of the beds and just falling down on it. The last conscious thought that Craig had before his eyes closed and sleep overcame him was the smiling face of his father looking at him from a picture, gray-green eyes locked on his.

# 6

Ft. Bragg, N.C.
9 May 1973

    He woke up slowly to the sound of children's voices somewhere in the house. Everything else was quiet and he lay on the bed for a while longer, enjoying the peace. He looked at his watch realizing that he had slept more than a couple of hours. He got up, searched for his bag and took out a change of clothes. Grabbing his toilet kit he opened the door and headed for the small bathroom. When he finished he came out feeling much better. He was ravenously hungry and wondered when he could get something to eat. Closing the bedroom door he walked around the small house, finding no one around. Somewhere close a radio could be heard, the sounds of Eric Clampton's voice coming to him clearly. Walking through the kitchen he opened the patio door, the smell of meat cooking on a charcoal grill assailed his nostrils. His mouth watered at the thought of food and he walked on the deck. Sitting on lounge chairs were Ragsdale and a blond woman. She was of medium height, a fair-skinned young woman slightly built. She looked to be in her thirties, but was in fact forty years old. Despite the fact that she had two children her body was still hard and lean, her breasts full and upright, straining against the cotton T-shirt she was wearing. A pair of short jeans showed her well-muscled and deeply tanned legs. At the sound of the door opening the woman looked up, giving Craig the opportunity to see her face. She had a pleasant face and eyes the color of amber, bright and shining. She had been in the middle of a sentence when the noise of the door opening caught her attention and upon seeing Craig emerging from the house, she got up. She stood still for a moment, her eyes locked on his.

"Oh my lord," she said, tears welling in her eyes, walking rapidly toward him. She embraced him, kissing his cheek softly, then taking a step backwards.

"I'm sorry," she said, running her hands over her eyes, "but you look so much like your father."

Craig's face turned deeply red and he stammered something, jamming his hands into his pockets.

Seeing his embarrassment, Ragsdale came to the rescue.

"This is my wife, Lynn," he said, putting his arm around her shoulders and pulling her close to him. At that moment there was the sound of children running and yelling and two girls came around the house chasing each other. Seeing their parents on the deck they stopped, their eyes fixed on the stranger. Shyly they came around, standing beside their mother. Craig smiled at them and that was too much for the youngest girl who proceeded to hide behind her mother. Looking at her Craig thought that she was probably the one on the phone the first time he had called, probably three or four years old. She was a beautiful child and it was easy to see that her looks were mostly from her mother while the oldest one had her father's eyes and smile.

"This is Samantha and Caroline," Ragsdale said, smiling at the children.

"Hi, girls," Craig said.

Samantha said hello, her face breaking into a shy smile while Caroline just grabbed her mother's leg, hiding her face.

"Come on kids," Lynn said, a grin on her face, "lets go in the house while daddy and Craig talk. Saying that she pulled Caroline away from her leg and with Samantha trailing her, they went into the house.

Ragsdale saw them go with a smile on his face. Craig could see by the look on his face that he was proud of his family.

"Come on and have a beer, Craig," Paul said, pulling two out of a cooler. He handed Craig one and then walked to the grill where several steaks were cooking. He checked the meat and then sat down next to Craig.

"Food will be ready shortly," he announced, taking a swig from the beer can. Craig looked at the sky noticing that the sun was almost gone. They talked about everyday things until Paul got up one more time to check on the meat and when he pronounced it ready, they transferred the steaks to a platter and carried the food inside. They ate at a small table sharing the food and making small talk. When they were finished, Ragsdale offered to help clean the table, but Lynn pushed them out.

"You men go outside," she said. "I'll bring coffee and apple pie later."

Kissing his wife on the cheek, Ragsdale walked outside, followed by Craig. "Sit down son," Paul said once they were outside. He pulled a cigar from a pack, offering one to Craig.

"No thanks," he said.

Paul nodded his head, lighting the cigar and puffing mightily on it. They were quiet for a while and then Ragsdale came straight to the point.

"Well, Craig," he said, looking at the young man sitting in front of him, "you came all the way from Boston to hear about your father and I'm glad you are here." He shook ashes from the cigar and continued talking. "Andrew Beck was my best friend and he shared with me the fact that he had a son, a son who he never knew he had until your Uncle Henry found him and told him about you. I knew him for over twenty years and I believe that I knew him better than anyone else. So if you are ready, I'll be glad to tell you what I know."

Craig Barlow got up from his chair and paced the length of the deck for a few moments. Darkness had come and the only light was from a small bulb on the wall.

Paul Ragsdale looked at the young man and waited until finally he stopped and faced him. His face was in shadows and his voice had an edge to it when he finally spoke.

"You know," Craig said, starting his pacing again, "I have been in almost complete shock since the moment I read that letter. All my life I was secure in the knowledge that I knew who I was, who my parents were, and my role in society." He paused for a minute coming to sit down by Paul and then he continued. "But after the letter nothing made any sense to me anymore. To find out that the man I thought was my father was not and that my mother had taken her knowledge of my real father to her grave was something that disturbed me greatly. After talking to my father and my uncle I thought I could put it to rest, but it was to no avail. My mind kept running like wildfire, wondering who this man was, what part of me was like him, what his life was all about, what he believed in." He was silent again, his face etched in deep thought. Paul waited, puffing on his cigar. He knew the boy was hurting, trying to decide if he really wanted to know more or just pack his bag and go home. The young man needed to come to terms with himself and make up his mind about Andrew Beck and what the man stood for. He drained his beer and waited patiently for the boy to continue. The next question would decide, Paul thought, getting up and grabbing another beer from the cooler.

When the questions came, it was nothing that he was expecting. "Were you there when he… when he died?" Craig asked a light tremor in his voice now.

"Yeah… I was there," Paul, said, surprised by the question. For a fleeting moment he was back in the jungle, the smell of cordite and the scream of men dying flooding his mind. In spite of the heat he shuddered, shaking his head to clear the bad memories.

"Yes, I was there," he murmured again so softly that he barely heard himself talking.

Craig noticed the change in the man and he remained silent, disturbed now at the emotions he had seen playing on Paul Ragsdale's face. They remained silent for a while; each one of them immersed in their own personal thoughts. Finally, Ragsdale fixed his eyes on Craig and spoke.

"Your father was a very special person, Craig," he said, taking a puff of the cigar. "He was my friend, he was a soldier and he was a brave man, a man who lived and died by some very simple words and principles. I don't know if I can do this, but if you want to know about him, I can try."

Craig remained silent for a few more seconds and then he spoke, his voice barely audible.

"Yes, Paul," he said. "I believe that I would like to hear about Andrew Beck."

# 7

Part II
The Man
Columbus, GA
19 October 1950

    The young man walking down the main street of Columbus, Georgia was tall, well over six feet. His shoulders were broad, tapering down to a small waist and long, slightly bowed legs, the result of a lifetime on horseback. His skin was burned to a dark brown by the sun and the wind and the overall appearance of the young man was one of incredible strength and endurance. His hair was jet black, cut short in military style. His face was young with a strong, square jaw and thin lips. He was a handsome young man in a rugged way and his gray-green eyes had a way of looking at the world around him like he was amused by it. Those same gray-green eyes could look at you and with one glance give you the impression that the man was not one to be taken lightly. Andrew Beck had been born in the hill country around Stonewall, Texas on January 19, 1927. The son of a top ranch hand and a beautiful Tex-Mex woman, he had lived his entire life on the Lazy B ranch where his father had worked for as long as he could remember. His mother had died in childbirth and the only memories he had of her were the old wrinkled pictures his father had kept of her in the old shack they used to live in. His father, Wesley Beck, had labored long and hard to raise him. He would get up while the stars still had a hold on the night sky to make the trip to his boss's small frame house to leave his son with Mrs. Fitzgerald while he and the boss took care of the ranch work. He had learned to ride a horse before he was able to walk and some of his earliest and fondest memories were of he and his father. He was all bundled up in blankets, riding with his father on horseback in the early hours of the morning. His father would talk to him and hold him tight so he wouldn't fall, his strong arms around him, his hand pointing at the stars while he made up stories about them. He had grown up on the ranch, sharing the harsh life of a cowhand with his father, learning the ropes and the wisdom that the hill country imparted to its inhabitants. It was a hard, lonely life, but he was happy with it, enjoying the wide-open spaces, the incredible blue sky and the rough work. While the harsh, rugged land of the hill country had shaped his body and spirit until he was tough and lean as whipcord, the lessons and words given him by his father had shaped his mind. Words like God, country, honor and duty were passed from father to son, until the young man came to the realization that those words were more than just words. In his father's simple way of life, those were words to live by, with God always first, followed closely by country and honor and always the call of duty. The harsh land they lived on was immense, making them humble and teaching respect for it, while at the same time getting them close to God. Young Andrew had learned his lessons well and just like his father, he had striven to live by those words.

His father was forty-two years old when the Japanese attacked the U.S. at Pearl Harbor and he was fifteen. Despite his age, Wesley had enlisted in the Army leaving Andrew with Mr. and Mrs. Fitzgerald. Shortly afterwards, his father had been sent to the Pacific and for two years the letters he send home had included far away names like Tarawa, Iwo Jima, and Philippines. Then one cold December day Wesley Beck came home, one leg shorter than the other due to a bullet that had destroyed his right knee. The old man never talked much about his wound, but every once in a while he would reminisce about his time in the army and he would take the old medals out, explaining to young Andrew what they were for. There had been a Purple Heart, and a shiny star that his father called a Silver Star among several other badges and medals. When that happened, young Andrew would go to bed and dream of far away lands and glorious battles that would etch a smile on his face while he slept.

His father was fifty years old when the accident occurred and he found himself completely alone in the world.

Wesley Back had been breaking broncos when the horse he had been riding crashed through the fence post, throwing Wesley to the ground. Unable to get up fast enough because of his crippled leg, Wesley lost precious seconds. He whirled around on the ground just in time to see the horse, crazy with pain and fear, lashing out at the form on the ground, its hooves crushing Wesley's skull. He had fought for a long time, but eventually his tired broken body finally gave up and Wesley Beck passed away. Andrew had been devastated, the death of his father and companion leaving an empty void in his heart that nothing could fill.

He had been absorbed in his pain when one day after burying his father he had heard the news. The U.S. was back at war, this time at a place called Korea. He had gotten up from his chair, finding an old atlas and searching for the place. It was far and he had never heard of it before. Slowly he had taken inventory of his prospects. He was twenty-three, almost broke, with no one to call family, living in a small shack in a place that was not his own and he decided to enlist in the army, thinking that maybe his country could use a man like him. It was his duty anyway, Andrew thought, remembering his father's lectures about the debt that every citizen had to pay for their freedom. Within days he had enlisted and had been on his way to Ft. Benning, Georgia for basic infantry training.

Regardless of what he had been thinking, army life was easy for him; the training and the long hours at the range were like child's play. The weeks had flown and he had taken to army life like a duck to water, finishing ahead of his class, especially in weapons qualifications where he had scored in the top range. All the years of hunting wild animals on the range for food had paid off and Andrew had earned the expert marksmanship badge, excelling with machine guns or any other kind of weapon that he was introduced to.

He had just finished his infantry training and was waiting for orders to Korea when he was given a fourteen-day leave prior to shipping out. He had thought about going to see the Fitzgeralds, but after a few minutes thought better of it. There was no sense in going back to Stonewall. He was sure the Fitzgeralds would be happy to see him, but they were not his family and in a couple of days he would be in their way. So he had stayed in Columbus, renting a motel room for two weeks. At this time there was plenty to do in town. There were people everywhere; the streets choked full of GIs. Bars were open to cater to them, while cars and trucks made in infernal racket that was torture to his ears after the silence he was used to back home.

He was dressed in jeans and cowboy boots and a long sleeve checked shirt that strained at the shoulders. On his head was his beloved black Stetson. He was out for a stroll before going to bed, his mind absorbing all the things going on around him, his eyes taking in the multitude of people going nowhere in a hurry.

He was just passing a dark alley to his left when his keen hearing detected some muffled yelps and curse words. For a second he hesitated, not wanting to get himself tangled up in something that wasn't his business, but then he heard someone yelling for help and throwing caution to the wind Andrew Beck entered the dark alley. In seconds his eyes adjusted to the dark and he could see several men, all in soldiers uniforms punching and kicking another form on the ground. There were three of them and Andrew waded in, his hard fists connecting with the skull of one, the man dropped to his knees. In seconds the other drunken GI realized that someone else had joined the fight and after several attempts to get the best of the young man they saw the futility of their efforts and ran away. Looking at the man on the ground Andrew bent over, pulling him by his arm, helping him to his feet.

"Are you okay, mister?" he asked, trying to peer in the darkness to assess the man's injuries.

"I'm... I'm fine," the man said, a painful gasp escaping his thin lips.

Andrew chuckled, his strong hands steadying the man. I don't think you are fine, mister," he said, pushing the man gently toward the entrance to the alley.

"We better get out of here before those friends of yours decide to come back with reinforcement," he said, walking and holding the man at the same time. They made it to the street, the soldier holding his ribs tenderly.

"I believe those bastards broke my ribs," he said wincing, his tone of voice clipped and precise. Andrew Beck looked at the soldier closely, wondering where the accent was from and then he realized that the soldier was an officer. A second lieutenant to be exact. The man was a mess and his tunic was filthy. There was blood on his lips where a fist had connected and an eye had already turned purple.

"I think you may need a doctor," he said, his hands still holding the man steady.

"I don't need a doctor," the clipped, precise voice said, pale blue eyes fixed on his. I'm sorry, I forgot my manners," the lieutenant said, his right hand coming up to shake hands with Andrew.

"My name is Henry Weatherly and I thank you for saving my life."

The young man in front of him just shrugged his shoulders, his gray-green eyes looking at the lieutenant, his right hand shaking the outstretched hand.

"I'm Andrew Beck," he said and then added, "private Beck, Sir."

The lieutenant in front of him tried a smile, wincing again at the pain.

"You can forget the Army formalities, Andrew," the man said, his hands brushing the filthy tunic, making the cloth look worse. He started walking and his knees wobbled, his body almost crashing to the sidewalk. Andrew saw the man begin to fall and he stepped in, his powerful hands reaching out and stopping the man's headlong fall.

"Whoa there mister," he said steadying the lieutenant. "I think you need a place to lay down."

The lieutenant shook his head to clear it, the pounding in his head making him sick. "Would you mind helping me to the USO Club?" he asked, steady on his feet once more.

"It's none of my business, Lieutenant, but I don't think you need a club right now," Andrew said, helping the man to walk.

"I'm sorry, I didn't explain," he said, looking at Andrew. "My sister… she is at the club working. If you just take me there she can take care of me." He shook his head slowly, wishing that the headache would go away.

Once again Henry Weatherly felt the young man's eyes on him and he looked up. The gray-green eyes were fixed on him, the look in them speculative, like the man was measuring him. For some unknown reason, Henry Weatherly felt that he wanted to meet the young man's approval, not wanting to be found inadequate in any way. He straightened himself up, squaring his shoulders, his head beginning to feel better with every breath he took. And he saw approval in the young man's eyes, his head nodding slightly at him.

"Come on, Lieutenant," Andrew said, his hand holding Henry Weatherly by the arm. Without another word they started walking, slowly at first and then more rapidly after the Lieutenant made it apparent that he was feeling much better. By the time they arrived at the USO they had shared bits and pieces of their lives, noticing how different their backgrounds were. Andrew Beck was from the hill country of Texas while Henry Weatherly was from Boston. One was penniless the other incredibly rich, but through their talk they soon found out that despite the fact that they were from different worlds they shared one thing in common. The words that Andrew Beck had heard so often from his father's lips, the words that were imprinted in his mind, were also part of this man walking by his side. He heard the lieutenant, a man just a few years older than him talking about God and country, honor and duty. By the time they made their way to the club, Andrew Beck felt that he had known the skinny second lieutenant forever.

Upon their arrival at the club it took Lieutenant Weatherly a few minutes to find his sister. They finally found her helping other staff members entertain a group of GI's at a card table. Andrew Beck stood in one place while Henry Weatherly walked the few steps to his sister and when he got her attention he saw the young girl stiffen perceptibly when she saw her brother's condition. They talked for a few minutes and then he saw the lieutenant pointing a finger in his direction, his sister looking at him, nodding her head. With a wave of his hand Henry Weatherly signaled private Beck to follow them and he started walking after them. Walking behind them, Andrew had an opportunity to really look at the Lt.'s sister and he felt his heart leap. Lord, but she was adorable, he said to himself, his eyes taking the lovely figure walking ahead of him. She was petit, slight of build, with shiny auburn hair, cut short. From the first look of her Andrew was smitten. They made their way into a small office, the young woman hovering close around the Lt.. She made him sit down and for the first time, she looked at Andrew, her eyes locked on his. For long seconds she held his eyes, and he marveled at the brightness of them. Her eyes were a pale shade of green, full of life and mischief and when she looked at him her face flushed deeply. She is beautiful, he thought again, seeing her small red lips and her flushed face. She walked toward him, her small hand extended and when he finally heard her voice his heart jumped again. For the first time in his young life Andrew Beck fell in love. Right then and there in a small office that he had never seen before, Andrew Beck felt his heart melt at the sight of the lovely woman in front of him and his eyes locked on hers again.

"My name is Catherine," she said, her accent like music to his ears. "Catherine Weatherly." Like in a daze, he shook her hand, his eyes fixed on her face. A smile flickered across her face and her eyebrows went up like she was asking a question. "Well?" she said, looking at him expectantly.

His face broke into a wide grin, realizing that she was waiting for him to tell her his name and he finally stammered "I'm sorry, mam," holding her warm soft hand with his while the other was busy with his hat. "My name is Andrew Beck and I'm pleased to meet you." She laughed then; a laugh full of merriment, like she was happy and then she turned her attention back to her brother, letting go of his hand. He let her go reluctantly feeling the emptiness that just letting go of her hand created. During all this her brother had been sitting quietly on the sofa, watching the play between them and he also laughed. He had seen men acting that way around his sister many times and he was glad that the cowboy was no different.

Catherine glanced at her brother for a few seconds and then walked to a small door at the side of the room.

"You are a mess, Henry," she said, opening the door and going in. In a few seconds, the sound of running water could be heard and shortly afterwards Catherine came out of the small bathroom holding a wet towel. Approaching her brother she started cleaning his face, slowly and tenderly. Andrew stood where he was just watching her, enjoying the way she moved and the sound of her voice.

"What happened to you?" she asked her brother while she worked, careful not to inflict more pain on him.

"I saw this GI that I thought was sick and when I approached him in this alley, two more men were there," Henry Weatherly said. "They said they wanted my money and when I refused they proceeded to kick the daylights out of me. I was lucky that my new friend Andrew was passing by, heard the commotion and decided to be a Good Samaritan and help me out of a mess."

She glanced at him still standing to the side and saw a smile come to his face. Once again their eyes locked and Andrew felt his heart running wild, wondering if the girl in front of him was feeling the same way.

When she finally finished cleaning her brother up they went back outside and for the rest of the evening they talked and shared things from their lives, getting to know each other better.

Andrew learned that Lt. Weatherly was in town just for a few days and that Catherine had come with two of her cousins to keep him company. In a few more days Henry would be leaving for good, heading for Korea just like him and Catherine would be going back to Boston.

For the next several days while Henry Weatherly was busy with bank business, Andrew kept Catherine busy and in the evening all of them got together. It wasn't long before Henry realized that the friendship that had developed between his sister and Private Beck had turned into something more serious and silently he felt sorry for them. He loved his sister dearly and didn't want anything painful to happen to her, but he knew that theirs was a lost cause. His father would never approve of Andrew Beck as a member of the family and all hell would break loose when he found out what Catherine was doing. In the end she would be the one to suffer and the one who would face his wrath. He liked the young man, had come to respect his wisdom and his outlook on life. He believed Andrew would go far, but he knew his father and he would never approve. So on his last day in Columbus he tried to talk to Catherine knowing damn well what her response would be. He knew her to be a strong woman but she was also obedient to her father's wishes and when the two of them came together, sparks would fly.

He had talked Catherine into taking him to the airport and while waiting for his plane to depart he found the time to talk to her. The two of them were alone, Andrew declining the invitation to go with them and saying his good-bye to Henry Weatherly while still in town .The sat at a small table , drinking coffee , waiting for the plane call and finally Henry Weatherly cleared his throat, looking at his sister .

"Catherine", he started, feeling like a louse about to spoil his sister's happiness.

"Catherine", he said again, "we must talk".

Catherine Weatherly looked at him, her brow creasing with worry lines at the tone in her brother's voice.

"What about?, she said, sipping her hot brew slowly, her eyes fixed on her brother's .

"About Andre Beck and you", he said, his face now serious.

Her eyes went to him again and she put the cup down. "What is wrong", she asked, waiting for him to continue.

"How serious is this between you and Andrew?"

"Pretty serious," she said. "Why?"

"I don't want to sound like I don't approve of you and Andrew, but I must warn you that our father… our father is really going to blow a fuse when he finds out about this."

She was silent for a while, mulling over his words. She finally looked at her brother, a deep sigh escaping her lips. When she spoke her lips trembled slightly and her eyes had lost their brightness.

"I love him, Henry," she said a sad smile flickering across her face. "I love him more than anything." She got up from the table hugging herself. The small terminal was chilly. It was the beginning of November and the weather was turning cold. It was almost midnight and the place was just about deserted, the only people around were the GIs who were about to depart for overseas. Catherine paced the small bar, finally coming back and sitting down heavily.

"I know what father is going to say, Henry, but I can't help the way I feel." She paused for a second her face becoming more animated as she talked about Andrew. "He makes me laugh, he makes me feel like a woman and he loves me." Henry Weatherly looked at his sister and his heart went out to her. Reaching across the table he held her hand.

"I like Andrew and nothing would please me more than to see the two of you together, but… but our father will never allow this to be."

"Why?" she asked. "Because Andrew's poor, because he is not from our society?" She was mad now, her eyes full of fury.

He didn't answer knowing well that his sister was aware of how their father would react when confronted with Andrew Beck and the reasons for it. He sat still sipping the rapidly cooling coffee. They remained silent for a moment, each one lost in their own thoughts.

"I know this is not fair but be careful, Sis," he said softly. "Our father is capable of some unspeakable things when he is angry."

Catherine Weatherly looked at her brother, tears running silently down her face and slowly nodded her head. At that moment the loudspeaker blared, calling for Henry's plane. With a deep sigh Henry got up, picked up his duffel bag and headed for the door to the plane.

They embraced quietly and then Henry Weatherly took a step back, his eyes bright. He tried to force a smile to his face, but only grimaced like a man in pain. Around them several GIs were passing by heading for the same plane that Henry would board, most of them alone, some with their wives or girlfriends clinging to them until the last moment.

With a swipe of her hand, Catherine Weatherly wiped the tears from her eyes. Her brother was going to war and he surely didn't need this, she thought trying hard to control herself.

"Be careful," she said, reaching over one more time and kissing her brother tenderly on the cheek. She stepped back to better look at him and then her eyes opened wide in amazement. She was twenty-two years old and in all her life she had never seen her brother cry, but now, standing in front of her she could see the tears brimming in his eyes. For a long moment he looked at her like a person trying to engrave her image in his mind. Without another word he whirled around, his shoulders sagging, a silent tear falling down his face. In a moment he was gone and Catherine Weatherly thought that she had never felt so alone in the world. With her heart aching she turned around wondering if she would ever see her brother alive again. She walked away her steps heavy, her thoughts on her brother's words. She knew well what her father would say and she trembled at the thought of hearing his voice, knowing what he was capable of when he was crossed. But she was willing to fight for Andrew and face the rage of her father for his love. Slowly she made her way, her shoulders slumped, and feeling like the whole world was lying on top of her.

# 8

Columbus, GA
2 November 1950

    She drove into town with her mind in a daze, her thoughts running wild. She didn't have any idea what she would tell her father, but she was sure that she was not going to spoil the last few days they had together by talking to Andrew about her father and his bigoted ideas. Money was nothing to her and she was pretty sure Andrew felt the same way, but her father was different. When she arrived at the boarding house where she and her cousins were staying, she went straight to her room. Her head was splitting and she was exhausted, completely drained from the conflicting emotions consuming her. Maybe everything would be fine, she thought, closing her eyes and praying for sleep, knowing well that sleep would be long in coming.
    The next morning found her in a better frame of mind and when it was time to meet Andrew, she tried to put on a good face. There was no need to let him see what a shape she was in. They only had three more days together before she was due back home and he was scheduled to

depart for Korea and his new assignment. She had spent the day with her cousins shopping and walking around town, waiting impatiently for the time to go by so she could be with Andrew. They were supposed to meet at a small restaurant on the outskirts of town and when she got there he was already waiting. She walked inside and saw him immediately, sitting at a small table for two. His face lit up the moment he saw her. He had on a new gray suit; a white shirt and a red tie complemented the attire. She thought that he was the most handsome man she had ever seen. He came to his feet when she approached the table, pulling out a chair for her. The place was small but crowded, mostly GIs in uniform and their dates and she felt right at home.

"Hi there," he said, his eyes lingering on hers, a smile pulling at the corners of his mouth. Her dress was a black silk affair that clung to her body like a glove, her pert breasts pushing against the fabric. Her face had just a trace of makeup and her small full lips were a cherry color that he found irresistible.

"Hi yourself," she said with a gaiety that she really didn't feel.

They made small talk until the waiter came by and took their orders. She was trying hard to be happy and lighthearted, but it was to no avail, her brother's words intruded in her mind. When the food came they picked at it, the silence between them lengthening with each passing moment. He finally put down his fork, reached across the table and took her small slender hand in his. She was so small, he thought, seeing her hand disappear in his.

"What's wrong?" he asked, his eyes dark and smoldering now. She had an incredible effect on him the moment he touched her and now was no different.

"I'm not very hungry," she said, her voice husky, almost a whisper.

They looked deep into each other eyes and Andrew thought he would die of longing for the woman sitting across from him. In the few days he had known her he had come to the realization that this was the woman for him, the one he had been waiting for all his young life. He was deeply and without a doubt in love with Catherine Weatherly, but he was not blind. He had seen her moods and her restrained silence more than once and he knew what was eating her. He was not a fool and even if he was not as sophisticated as she was it wasn't hard for him to read between the lines. But he was not going to be the one to bring the subject of their differences to a head. He couldn't care less if she was rich or poor, his love for her would always be the same.

He saw her face tilt to the side, a crooked smile began to appear in what was a characteristic gesture for her when she was being mischievous and her hold on his hand tightened. When she spoke it was just a whisper and he almost missed what she said.

"Let's get out of here," she said. "I want to make love to you."

"What...what did you say?" he asked, believing that he had misunderstood her words.

She didn't answer, getting up and looking at him. There was more in that look than in a thousand words. Andrew dropped some bills on the table and slowly, in a daze, they made their way out to Catherine's car. They drove in silence until they reached his motel room.

The moment the door closed behind them Andrew reached for her, his lips finding hers in a long, searching kiss. Her lips were soft and her tongue inside his mouth drove him crazy with desire. He crushed her to him, his manhood standing stiff and felt her grind against him, a muffled sound escaping from her lips. She felt his hands on her dress pulling it off and then his fingers were busy with the rest of her clothing, while his mouth and lips were all over her. He stopped for a second, looking at her in the light filtering through the small window and his breath caught in his throat at the sight of her.

"You are beautiful," he said, his eyes lingering on the small, high breasts, going down to the dark, triangle patch of hair between her legs. He undressed hurriedly and gently he pushed her down on the bed. The next thing she knew he was inside her and for a second there was pain and then she was caught up in a wild orgy of passion that threatened to overwhelm her with its intensity. She reached for him, enjoying the softness of his skin and at the same time, the hardness of his incredible muscular body. And then she was over the edge, her whole body trembling, moans escaped from her lips until she shuddered and lay quietly against him, spent, her breath coming in ragged gasps while her heart beat a wild tempo.

They lay side by side until their breathing was normal and then he raised his head on one elbow and looked at her tenderly, his eyes bright.

"Are you all right?" he asked, concern in his voice.

"Just slightly sore down there," she answered, "but happy." She was quiet for a few minutes, her head against his powerful chest, listening to his heartbeat. "This was my first time."

"Mine too," he said and she was glad that she had waited.

Andrew laughed a happy laugh and then he started touching her, his hands and fingers caressing her while his eyes roamed over her body. Slowly she felt her heart racing again and she dropped her hand to his crotch finding him stiff. Gently he turned her over and made love to her again until the stars exploded in front of their eyes and their cries mingled with each other, their bodies and soul immersed completely in the moment. Like in a dream, he heard her calling his name over and over until she gave a small gasp and shuddered beneath him.

For the next two days they stayed at the motel, eating, sleeping and making love until on the third day it was time for Andrew to leave. He would be heading for San Francisco and then Japan and finally Korea. She would be going home the same day with her cousins. She had given him her address and he had promised to write. They made their way to the airport in silence, their hearts heavy at the prospect of being apart. The weather was getting cold and the sky was overcast, adding to their gloomy thoughts. Arriving at the terminal Andrew checked his baggage at the counter and came back to her. He was dressed in his Army uniform this time, cutting an impressive figure. From where she was standing Catherine could see several women looking at him as he went by and she smiled. He was a handsome devil, she thought, glad that he was hers.

"I'm getting good at good-byes," she said when Andrew came to stand by her side. He nodded his head knowing that she was referring to her brother's departure a few days before. And like before, the place was full of GIs headed overseas and their families. They made small talk for a while, neither one of them saying what was on their mind until finally the plane call came. Andrew got up, his eyes locked on hers. Reaching over he touched her face gently with his fingers.

"I love you, Catherine," he said, a smile flickering across his face, his gray-green eyes sad at the impending separation.

"I love you too, cowboy," she said, trying to make light of the moment.

He stared at her for a short time and then he shook his head and smiled at her. Without a word he hefted his duffel bag and with a final, all encompassing look at her, he turned around and headed for the waiting plane. She followed him with her eyes until he entered the airplane waiting on the tarmac, her heart beating wildly, an awful premonition that she would never see him again haunting her.

# 9

Columbus, GA
Pan American Flight #278
5 November 1950

    The plane Andrew boarded in Columbus, GA., was a brand new Pan American DC-6 and in a few minutes it was completely full of GIs. He scanned the faces drifting by but was not able to recognize any of them. He sat quietly next to a window and idly contemplated the sea of humanity coming into the plane. Some of the faces were young; fear and excitement etched on them and others were not so young, their faces serious, wondering what lay ahead of them. He closed his eyes, daydreaming, thinking about Catherine, oblivious now to the din in the aircraft until he was brought out of his reverie by a hand on his shoulder. He opened his eyes at the touch to see a tall, fair skinned GI with broad shoulders smiling at him. The soldier looked to be about eighteen, but was in fact almost twenty, his face still showing traces of acne. He had short, blond hair and blue eyes in a friendly face.

"This seat taken?" he asked with a grin on his face as he looked down at Andrew. His voice was flat, non-committal and Andrew couldn't place his accent. He had made it a game since coming to basic training to try and figure out where the myriad of GIs he came in contact with were from by identifying their accents. More often than not he was able to come up with the right area of the country they were from.

He looked at the soldier standing on the aisle and couldn't help but smile to himself. "No... no," he answered, "come on and sit down," reaching for the overcoat that he had dropped on the seat next to him.

The soldier sat down, buckling his seat belt and then looked around the plane at all the activity, finally settling down in his seat.

"Just like a heard of cattle heading for the butcher shop," he said, shaking his head.

Andrew heard the comment and thought how appropriate it was for the occasion, but didn't say anything, just nodded his head. He really was in no mod for small talk and it appeared to him that his new seat companion was a talker. He closed his eyes to discourage conversation, but was jolted out of his private thoughts by his companion.

"I'm Paul J. Ragsdale," the man sitting next to him said and Andrew opened his eyes to see the fellow extending a hand to him. Giving up on the idea of keeping to himself, Andrew shook the proffered hand.

"Andrew Beck," he said, noticing the strength in the fellow's hand.

They made small talk for a few minutes while all around them the hum of conversation could be heard. He found out that the young man was from Seattle, Washington and, like himself, had just come into the Army and was assigned to the 19th Infantry Regiment in Korea. Eventually they both fell silent, each one lost in their own private thoughts until Paul J. Ragsdale fell asleep in his seat.

In a few more minutes the plane was completely full and shortly thereafter the propellers started and the plan was taxiing down the runway, becoming airborne. Andrew settled himself in his seat, looked around one more time and before long had closed his eyes, sleep overtook him also.

They woke up when the plane landed for refueling and shortly afterward the plane took off again, finally landing in San Francisco.

Several Army buses were waiting for them at the terminal and shortly after deplaning they were taken to a mess hall where they were fed and given the opportunity to clean up some. After that it was back on another plane. An Air force cargo plane this time for the flight to Honolulu, Hawaii and then another plane ride for Tokyo, Japan. By the time they arrived in Japan they were bushed, their brains mushed. They were met at the airfield in Japan by more buses with some name that Andrew couldn't read printed on the side. Then they were transported to an Army barracks for the night, the NCO (non-commissioned officer) in charge calling names from a master roster and assigning GIs together according to the unit they had been assigned to. While at the Army camp they were issued footlockers for their gear they would be leaving behind and then they were issued their web gear, fatigues, combat boots and cold weather gear, including field jackets and finally steel pots and their rifles. After the long trip, Andrew and Paul had become fast friends and the two of them found they were assigned to the same barracks, bunking together for the night.

"Well, it would be nice if we could both get assigned to the same company," Paul said, digging in his duffel bag, his head halfway inside it. Andrew was busy taking some toilet articles out of the bag and it was a few seconds before he raised his head to find the Sergeant in charge standing by their bunk. The soldier was a Sergeant First Class (an E-7), a man of medium height with short-cropped hair. The man's eyes were tired and red rimmed and he was looking at Andrew Beck with a speculative look. He wore Army fatigues and a field jacket—everything starched and pressed. His boots were clean and shiny and the man exuded professionalism. On the right side of his jacket was his nametag and on the left, above U.S. Army, the paratrooper's badge could be seen. Right above the paratrooper's badge was a CIB (Combat Infantryman's Badge) with one star above it denoting a second award.

"You are PFC Andrew Beck," the Sergeant said, making it more of a statement than a question.

Andrew Beck came to attention at the same time that he answered.

"Yes, Sergeant," he said, his voice loud inside the confines of the barracks. "I'm Private Beck."

The old, grizzled Sergeant approached him, his eyes taking the young man in. "Stand at ease, soldier," he said, and waited until Andrew dropped the position of attention.

"Is your father by any chance Wesley Beck?" he asked, his tired eyes fixed on Andrew.

Andrew's face tightened at the name of his father, wondering how the man in front of him had known him.

"Yes…he was killed by a bronco a few months ago," Andrew explained, the memory of his father's death still fresh in his mind.

The old Sergeant finally smiled and shook his head. He sat down on one of the bunks and stretched out his legs. He was fifty-one years old, not as young as he used to be and it had been a long day so far.

"Your father was a good soldier, son," he said. "He was with me at a place called Corregidor and he saved my life."

Andrew Beck looked at the weather beaten face of the old soldier sitting close to him and then he looked at the nametag on his chest, Williams. The Sergeant saw him looking and a smile flickered across his face.

"My name is Stanley Williams," he said, waiting for any indication that the young man had heard the name before.

"I bet your father never talked about me," he continued, "but then, your father was the most unassuming individual I have ever met and he didn't like talking much at all."

Williams reached in his pocket and brought out a pack of cigarettes, offering one to each of them and lighting up. He stretched his right hand, picking a butt can half filled with water from the nearby footlocker and set it down next to him. Andrew accepted the cigarette thinking that he needed to quit the damn habit. He had started smoking during basic training and Catherine had fussed about it constantly.

Listening to the Sergeant's words Andrew's face broke into a grin, knowing that what the Sergeant was saying about his father was the truth.

"Yes, you are right, that's just the way he was," he said, smiling now at the memories.

They talked for a while and Andrew Beck found out that his father had saved this man's life at the same time that he had been wounded in the leg.

"We went through hell in the Pacific, son, but your father never complained, never shirked his duty," he said, finally getting up. He cleared his throat and then fixing his eyes on Andrew, he continued.

"Your father was one of the good ones," he said, shaking his head. "He should have gotten the Medal of Honor for what he did that night, not just the Silver Star." He gathered his clipboard and put on his hat.

"I'm glad you are in this one, son, just be careful." He lit another cigarette, drawing deeply and exhaled slowly, the smoke drifting lazily upwards, making him close one eye.

He glanced around one more time and then he continued. "We are not ready for this war," he said, more like he was talking to himself than to them. "We are short of men, short of supplies and equipment and the damn bureaucrats won't get off their asses." He paused for a second, the cigarette dangling from his lips. "Our only hope is MacArthur." He stopped again, shaking his head.

"So what I'm telling you guys is to take care of yourself and learn fast."

He looked at his list again and then he looked at Paul J. Ragsdale. The young man was looking at him intently, wondering what the old

Sergeant was about to do. "You are both assigned to the same Regiment so how about the same company?" he asked, smiling now.

"That would be great, Sergeant Williams," Andrew said, fixing his eyes on the old warrior. "And thanks."

"Get some sleep guys," he said. "I'll be here early in the morning for the last leg of your trip."

The Sergeant looked at Andrew one more time, nodded his head and walked away. Andrew saw him go, a part of him wanting to follow the man, to talk with him and learn more about his father, but he thought better of it. The old Sergeant was probably tired and wouldn't want to be bothered this late.

Sergeant Williams walked out of the barracks, his mind on the young man he had just talked to. It was ironic that after all these years he had come face to face with the son of the man who had saved his life so many years ago, and he was going to the butchering fields of Korea, he thought, shuddering at the memories. He had just come from there and was on his way back again, as a matter of fact, with a new bunch of men. More than half of which would be dead in less than two weeks. He found the Sergeant in charge of the company clerks typing orders and paused by his desk.

"Johnny, do me a favor," he said, reaching for his clipboard. "Put Private Beck and Private Ragsdale together in the same company. Cut the orders today and let me have them in the morning."

"Sure Sergeant, no problem," the man said, taking the clipboard from Williams' hands and checking the names. "What's up?" he asked after he had finished with the names.

"The Beck boy," he said, chewing thoughtfully on his lower lip, "he is the son of an old friend. I owe him."

They talked quietly for a few more minutes and finally Williams made his way to his bunk. He was tired from the long day of baby-sitting a new bunch of GIs and was glad that they would reach their destination by tomorrow. He undressed and climbed in his bed, feeling his body beginning to relax, his mind drifting. The last thought that crossed his mind before sleep overcame him was of a jungle clearing his body recoiling at the pain in his right shoulder from a mortar fragment and the man who had carried him to safety, braving enemy fire, almost loosing his own life to save him.

# 10

Tokyo, Japan
6 November 1950

    Andrew Beck woke up to complete silence. He laid still, his eyes closed, enjoying the warmth under his blanket. He opened his eyes realizing that it was still dark outside. Silently he dropped to the floor from the top bunk, glancing at Ragsdale snoring softly in his bunk. He started to get dressed when he saw movement at the entrance to the barracks. Two men came in, stopping briefly to talk with the fireguard. One of the men reached to the side picking up the lid of a trashcan. Walking down the center isle the man flipped the lights and immediately started banging the metal lid while yelling loudly at the same time.

    "Okay people, get up, get up, get up!" he yelled at the top of his lungs. "Get your dicks on the floor and let's go." He banged on the metal lid several more times and finally seeing that most of the GI's were dragging themselves out of the beds he stopped and walked back toward the entrance, joining the other man there. Within minutes, the whole place was crawling with GI's going back and forth to the latrines and getting dressed.

Andrew finished dressing and stood aside waiting for Paul J. Ragsdale. He raised his eyes in time to see SFC Williams walking down the center of the barracks making sure that everyone was up and in the process of getting ready to go.

"Listen up people," he said, stopping in the middle of the isle waiting until the noise had subsided. "We will be leaving shortly so be in formation in two minutes."

With that he whirled around exiting the building. In less than two minutes the barracks was empty and shortly after that busses arrived to take the replacements to a mess hall. After that they were bussed again for the trip to the terminal and an hour later, 0600 hours, they were boarding a cargo plane for Korea. The weather was awful, cold and raining, making the long journey miserable. The plane shook and bumped all the way and several GIs started throwing up, making everyone sick.

Eventually they arrived in Korea, Pusan to be exact and once again they were told to get in formation. It was raining a slow steady drizzle that had them soaking wet in no time. The GIs shuddered at the cold, their breath coming out in clouds. Several Army 'douce and a half' ton trucks were parked next to the formation, the engines on and the windows closed tightly, the drivers smoking or catnapping—waiting. Andrew looked around seeing SFC Williams approaching the formation. While waiting for the rest of the people to form Williams came to stand by Andrew offering him a cigarette.

Andrew accepted gratefully, lighting up and drawing the smoke deep into his lungs. For a few seconds Williams was silent and then facing Andrew he started talking.

"You be careful out there son," he said, "and keep your eyes open." He took another drag of the cigarette looking at the troops. He shook ashes on the ground and then put the cigarette out with his fingers, putting the butt in his pocket.

"I'll be heading in another direction soon," he said, water falling from the brim of his hat, "so take care". He extended his right hand shaking Andrew's hand with a strong grip and without preamble, walked away.

The NCO in charge called names again grouping the soldiers by companies this time and in a few short moments everyone was ready to go. Andrew looked around noticing that there were about fifteen people in his group. Paul was one of them. They smoked until it was time to get on the trucks and within seconds they were moving. Andrew looked around seeing a myriad of emotions displayed on the faces of the young men in the truck. Most were apprehensive, all the banter and joking gone now, giving way to some serious thoughts and where they were and what they were about to do. This was war, Andrew thought, and people die in wars and they better be ready for it, because death does not wait for anyone.

They huddled inside the cramped interior of the truck for two hours, bouncing all over the uneven road until after what seemed an eternity, the truck stopped with a lurch, gears grinding.

Andrew got up, his legs stiff, the cold sipping slowly into his body. Damn, its cold he thought, tightening his jacket around him. And this was just November, he thought again, wondering what it would be like later on.

They jumped out of the truck, milling around, looking at their new surroundings, until a buck sergeant (E-5) came to get them. Soldiers could be seen here and there, but for the most part the place was empty. They were in the middle of some valley, void of any trees or vegetation, with several bunkers and tents serving as living areas and command post. Smoke spiraled in the air from stoves inside the tents and a sign in front of a large bunker read: U. S. Army, Able Company, 19th Infantry Regiment

They were home, sweet home.

The Sergeant put them in formation, gave them the word at ease, and walked away, disappearing inside the bunker. For a few seconds the replacements were left on their own, looking around at the dreadful conditions and then an officer and the buck Sergeant came out of the bunker.

"Atten-hut," the buck Sergeant said, stopping in front of the formation. There were fifteen of them and they all looked expectantly at the two men.

The officer looked at them closely shaking his head slowly. He was a short, stocky framed man with sandy color hair, cut short. His eyes were dark brown, large and intelligent.

"I'm Captain Cherry," he said, walking in front of the men, his eyes measuring them one by one, "your company commander. On behalf of the 19th Infantry Regiment, I welcome you. We are glad you are here, we need you desperately." He stopped talking and walked all around the new replacements, checking gear and weapons.

"This is Sergeant Walker, your platoon sergeant and acting 1st Sergeant," he said, his head pointing in the direction of Sergeant Walker. "He will teach you the ropes and take care of all your needs. We will be moving in the morning to an area south of here, so take care of your gear and if you have any questions, see your Sergeant."

With that he turned around leaving the men to Sergeant Walker. He stopped just before the entrance to the CP and looked back at the men he had just inspected. They are so young, he thought, and inexperienced. Most of them would be dead before the month was over. He sighed deeply, wishing there was more he could do, but he was short of men and equipment and officers. He had one platoon leader left, the others had been killed in a skirmish less than two days ago. He was also short on non-commissioned officers and didn't even have a 1st Sergeant anymore. He shook his head and with a last look at the men, went inside the bunker.

Sergeant Walker spent the next hour splitting the fifteen replacements among the four platoons and once again Andrew and Paul J. Ragsdale were put together, members of the 1st platoon. They spent the rest of the miserable day cleaning equipment and their personal gear, freezing in the cold. That evening their meal consisted of C-rations, the men grumbling about it while eating it and the sleeping quarters was a tent for four men. Sometimes during the early hours of the morning, a hand on Andrew's shoulder woke him up and a whisper told him that it was time for guard duty. He had gone to sleep in his clothes just pulling his boots off and it was just a matter of minutes before he was ready, leaving the rest of the men inside the tent snoring softly.

Once outside he was shown where he was supposed to keep guard and the soldier disappeared, leaving him alone for the night. He looked at his watch with the help of a flashlight with a red cover on the lens, noticing that it was four in the morning. He looked at the cloudless sky full of stars. The rain had stopped but it was still cold and silent. After a while he didn't feel the cold anymore, his mind relegating the discomfort to a subconscious level. He had learned that trick from his father and had practiced it when hunting for food, withstanding the cold and the rain stoically for hours. He walked around slowly to keep his blood moving, his mind on the woman he had left behind, wondering what would happen to them. He daydreamed of her with one part of his mind, the other focusing on the task at hand, until the first hint of daylight appeared on the horizon, the Company coming awake. Sergeant Walker appeared out of nowhere and told him to get some chow. They would be leaving at 0700 hours for the new post. Hurrying now he gulped his breakfast and finding a spot that was fairly deserted he sat down to write a letter for Catherine. God only knew when he would have the time to write again, he thought, trying to focus on the words. He filled the pages, put his address down and asked her to write soon. Then he sealed it and dropped it into the outgoing mail basket at the Command Post. After that he found Paul and together they finished their packing, ready for whatever was coming next.

A pale sun had come out but it was still cold and soon, the dark, rolling clouds came back and then the rain, making everything wet and miserable again. Within the hour they were ready to roll and slowly, like an awakening snake the Company moved, heading south and to their destiny, the dirt road turning into mud in a short time the men grumbling, their eyes haunted, wondering what was waiting for them around the next bend.

# 11

Brookline, Boston
15 November 1950

While her lover was fighting for his life on the frozen ground of Korea, Catherine Weatherly was about to start a battle of her own. She sat in her bedroom, the door closed, her mind mulling over the fact that she had been sick to her stomach for the past week. It had been two weeks since she came back from Columbus, GA and for the past few days her stomach had been in turmoil every morning. Today had been no different and she was nervous, believing that she knew what was going on. She was pregnant, she thought, the idea bringing a smile to her face, making her think of Andrew. She had not received a letter from him yet but she knew that he was in a dangerous place and she needed to be patient. He probably didn't have much free time on his hands, just like her brother, Henry, she thought, going about getting dressed. It was early in the morning, barely nine and Carlotta would be knocking on the door with her breakfast anytime. She finished dressing and opened the door, starting to walk downstairs. She was almost at the bottom when Carlotta made her appearance, a heavy tray in her hands.

"Where are you going child?" she said, her huge brown eyes looking over Catherine.

"I'm going out, Nana," she said, stopping to inspect the tray. She wasn't hungry, her stomach still queasy. She picked up a piece of toast, smiled at Carlotta and planted a big wet kiss on her cheek as she walked past.

"You come back here right now child," she heard Carlotta's voice behind her. She stopped, whirled around and came back.

"I'm not hungry, Nana," she said, looking at Carlotta.

"Child, you haven't been hungry since you came back from that place," she said looking at Catherine with a suspiciously. "What's going on?"

Catherine Weatherly looked around, her hands twisting and then she made up her mind. Taking hold of Carlotta's hand she pulled her to her side and looked her in the eyes.

"I need to talk to you anyway," she said. "Come upstairs with me please."

Carlotta looked at the woman child in front of her and saw the anguish etched on her young face and her heart jumped, wondering what kind of trouble she was in.

"Oh Lord, oh Lord," she said, flustered now. "What is wrong child?" she asked, her huge frame beginning to shake.

"Come on, Nana, let's go to my room."

They climbed the stairs and upon reaching Catherine's room Carlotta placed the tray on a table and sat down heavily on the bed, waiting, her eyes bewildered.

Catherine came to sit by her, taking her hand. She looked at Carlotta, her kind eyes, her round face full of worry lines now and she knew that Carlotta would be able to help her, no matter what.

"You know," she started, picking her words carefully, "that young man I met in Columbus—Andrew?"

"Yes child, I know. That's all you have talked about for the past two weeks," Carlotta said, her heart beginning to beat faster. She had been with the Weatherly family all her life and her parents before that. She had seen this child for the past week not eating, the worried look on her face and she had seen the bathroom. She cleaned it every day, not allowing any of the other help to come in Catherine's room. She had raised this child since she was a little baby and thought of Catherine as her own. And she knew that she was pregnant. She held the young woman's hand and squeezed it tightly, waiting.

"Nana, I think I'm pregnant," she said, fear and elation in her voice now.

"Oh child, oh child," she said as silent tears started falling down her plump cheeks.

"I'm scared, Nana," she said, embracing the woman in front of her, trying to draw strength from her. "What am I going to do."?

Both women held onto each other until Carlotta pushed her gently away, looking into Catherine's tear stained face.

"You must tell your father, child," she said, knowing full well that old man Weatherly would go crazy the moment he heard his daughter was pregnant. Carlotta had heard enough about young Andrew Beck to realize the man was not exactly what Robert Weatherly would like for his daughter and she had known the old man long enough to know what would happen when Catherine talked to him.

"I'm afraid, Nana," Catherine said. "My father is going to be mad."

Carlotta nodded her head, thinking that the man would be more than mad, and at that time she was afraid for this child, knowing well that Robert Weatherly could be very mean and cruel when someone crossed him.

"Where is he?", Catherine asked, drying her tears.

"He is in the study child", she said, wiping her own tears with her apron.

Catherine sighed deeply and then she got up, a shy smile on her face.

"Well, this is as good a time as any," she said, a determined look on her young face now.

Carlotta saw her go, her heart breaking, knowing full well that Robert Weatherly would not take kindly to what was coming.

Silently she got up and went back downstairs. She needed to find Benjamin. Maybe the two of them together could find a way of helping their child.

Catherine knocked on her father's door, listened for a second and then pushed the door open. She knew her father didn't like to be bothered while he was in the study. He was usually working and became annoyed when he was interrupted, but she felt this was important.

She walked in to find her father on the telephone, his voice loud, his face red. She was about to turn around and go when she saw his hand go up in the air, beckoning her in. She inhaled deeply and took two steps into the room, closing the door softly behind her. She stood still while he finished his conversation, waiting while she realized that it was the wrong time for this talk. But it was too late now, she was resolved to get this over with.

Robert Weatherly, III, was a big man, well over six feet tall. He was forty-eight years old with a ruddy complexion and a strong face with a high-domed forehead. His mouth was a dry line and his eyes were a dull, grayish-brown, hard and inscrutable at times. His hair, already receding, was a sandy color, perfectly combed. He was fully dressed in an expensive brown three-piece suit. The man exuded power and wealth and in the business community he was well known for his ruthlessness. While the firm of Weatherly & Weatherly had been in the black when he took over from his father, now it was really booming, their business increasing by leaps and bounds, even going international.

Finishing his phone business, Robert Weatherly slammed the phone down, the expression on his face one of utter contempt. He looked at his daughter and brusquely asked, "What do you want?" He didn't wait for an answer, getting up and selecting a cigar from a closed box on his desk. Cutting the tip with a pair of gold scissors he lit the Cuban cigar, inhaling the smoke deeply into his lungs.

"Well," he asked again, his eyebrow rising in question, letting the smoke out in small circles.

Catherine took a deep breath and forged ahead, her heart beating wildly, dreading what was coming.

"I… I met this young man, father," she started, seeing the expression on her father's face change gradually as she spoke. "His name is Andrew Beck and he is in the Army right now and…," Catherine stopped herself, her body beginning to tremble at the look on her father's face. He looked at her, his eyes narrow with disdain and then he spoke, "And who is this Andrew Beck?" he asked, his voice neutral now. "I don't recognize his name. Is he a new acquaintance?"

She was silent for a second, her mind running like wildfire and then she continued.

"He is the man I love, father and I want you to know about him."

For a second her father didn't react to the news, his eyes cold now, and his nostrils contracting reflexively.

"So you are in love," he said derisively, more a statement than a question. "Tell me all about it, Catherine."

She shook her head yes and then continued, her words gushing out now, afraid that if she stopped she wouldn't be able to continue. By the time she finished she was out of breath, her cheeks flushed and she waited, wondering what her father's reaction would be to the news that she was pregnant and in love with a penniless cowboy.

And the reaction was not long in coming. Robert Weatherly had listened to his only daughter with fascination, his mind wondering all the time how any child of his could do such a thing and when it was over he looked at her with such a look of disgust that Catherine shrank away. She saw her father get up from his leather chair and come to stand just inches away from her. He looked at her as one would look at a cockroach, needing to be stepped on and killed. Then he said, "Catherine Weatherly, you are insane, coming in here to tell me this trash." He stopped for a second, his eyes on her and then he continued, his voice becoming louder and louder by the second, his face flushed deep red, spittle flaying from his mouth.

"You are out of your mind, damn you girl…bringing dishonor and shame to me, to my name." He started pacing the office, screaming now, his face livid with mortification. "I'll see you dead before you even think about marrying a penniless cowboy from damn Texas, or wherever the hell he's from," he said, his arms flailing in the air, his eyes wild.

Catherine made as if to speak and he pounced on her, screaming, his face inches from hers.

"Shut up, damn you, shut up. I don't want to hear another word uttered in my house about this." He paused then, chewing on his cigar, sweat dripping from his forehead. At that time the door opened and Susan Weatherly, Catherine's mother came into the study, a look of concern on her face. She was a small woman, petit and quite distinguished looking, every inch the rich, sophisticated lady. Her hair was short, a light brown and her eyes were the color of amber, clear and intelligent. Hearing the door open Catherine looked up, seeing her mother come in. She whirled around, reaching her mother and hugging her fiercely, hoping that her mother would understand.

"Susan, you better talk to your daughter," Robert Weatherly said, looking at his wife. "She is going crazy, talking about having some damn cowboy's child and getting married."

Her mother looked at her with something like wonderment on her face and then she said, "What in God's name is going on in here?"

Robert Weatherly sneered and proceeded to tell his wife all that had transpired. "It looks like our daughter took advantage of our good will to go and get herself pregnant by some GI while she was in Georgia," he finished, his lips curling in disgust at the thought.

Catherine was sobbing, her heart beating wildly and her head splitting. The towering rage engulfing her father was like nothing she had ever seen and she trembled like a reed in a high wind.

She was hoping that her mother would take her side, but her hopes were dashed. "I can't believe that you would do something like that child," her mother said, pushing Catherine away from her, a stern look on her face.

Her father approached her and putting his face close to hers he said, "I want this bastard child of yours aborted, Catherine, or I'll make your life a living hell."

Catherine looked at her parents and she shook her head wondering how she could be their child. With tears streaming down her face she faced her father. "I'm not going to abort this child father," she said, her voice trembling, her eyes defiant. "I don't care what you do to me, I'm having Andrew's baby." She held his eyes for a moment longer and then she ran out, her heart in her mouth, fear and revulsion making her weak. Outside, Carlotta was waiting, tears streaming down her face and the two women embraced, holding each other tenderly.

"Come child, come," Carlotta said softly, her heart also breaking.

Inside the study Robert Weatherly was still full of rage and disgust. He walked to the door of the study reaching for his hat and jamming it on his head.

"Susan, you better talk some sense into that girl or she is going to wreck our reputation."

"Don't worry, dear," Susan Weatherly responded, "we will find a solution to this mess."

Robert Weatherly exited the study, leaving his wife with a determined look on her face. On his way out he found Benjamin and stopped to talk to him.

"Benjamin, from now on, I want all the mail picked up by you and brought to my desk every evening," he said, putting his overcoat and gloves on while he talked. "Is that understood?" he asked, fixing his cold hard eyes on Benjamin.

"Yes sir," Benjamin said, lowering his eyes to the ground.

From that day on with the combined will of both parents against her, Catherine Weatherly found herself besieged by threats, her will tested to the limits. But it was a losing battle. Without moral support, except for

Carlotta, and with her brother away, Catherine found herself isolated, pushed to the edge by her father's power, threatening to cut her out of her inheritance. And no letters from Andrew, or at least she thought that he had not written. Unknown to her the mail was delivered to her father and he in turn made sure that any letters from Korea were from his son, any others discarded.

At the end of two weeks when she was again summoned to the study to face her parents, she was at the end of her rope, dejected and depressed. She knocked on the door and quietly went in, seeing her parents waiting for her. The first words from her father surprised her and then threw her into a whirlpool of desperation.

"Your mother and I have decided that since you want to have that bastard child, then you can have it," he said. He stopped, the smoke from his cigar curling in the air, drifting slowly. "But you are going to have to marry Oliver Barlow."

She was caught off guard by her father's words and looked at him with a look of surprise on her face.

"And what makes you think Oliver Barlow would marry me?" she asked, wondering what was going on now.

"I have talked to Oliver and he has agreed to give his name to the damn child if you marry him."

She was silent for a minute, her brain tired as it was, thinking about what her father had just said. What was Oliver getting out of this she thought, pondering the implications. Oliver had been after her for years, but she didn't love him, thinking of him as just a friend. And now her father had arranged for him to marry her, giving her child his name.

"Why would he do that?" she asked, looking steadily at her father, seeing him fidgeting.

He cleared his throat and then he answered her. "I've agreed to make him a full partner in the firm."

"Well, so that's his price," she said, sarcasm heavy in her voice. "He gets me and a partnership in the firm in exchange for his good name."

She looked around, bewildered, sitting down heavily on a sofa. Tears were rolling down her face, her sobs shaking her slender frame. For a while silence reigned in the study, broken only by Catherine's crying. She finally stopped, her eyes swollen, her shoulders slumped. In a tired and broken voice she addressed her parents.

"I'll think about this proposition and give you an answer tomorrow," she said, walking slowly away, a dejected, beaten figure.

The next day her father got the answer he wanted and within two weeks Catherine had been married to Oliver Barlow by a justice of the Peach, a friend of her father's. Shortly afterwards the newlyweds departed for Europe, planning on a long stay.

Carlotta and Benjamin had seen them go and their hearts had been sad for the child, while Robert Weatherly and his wife congratulated themselves. With any luck the bastard child would be born in Europe and no one would be the wiser. He had enough money and influence to see that everything was taken care of and the honor and good name of the family would be protected.

# 12

Able Company, 19th Infantry Regiment
Near Hangnyong, South Korea
22 November 1950
0300 hours

    Andrew Beck sat on his haunches on the cold ground fifty meters in front of the bunkers, his M1-Garand rifle cradled in his arms, listening to the night sounds. For the past two weeks the company had tried their best to make the small hills they had secured a defensive position. The ground had been frozen most of the time and the bunkers and trenches had taken forever to build. Even now, after two weeks, the place was nowhere near finished and during his first visit the battalion commander, Lt. Colonel Devlin, in a brisk business-like voice had let it be known that they needed to get on with the program. Companies Able and Baker had been assigned the job of holding the hills at all cost and there would not be a retreat. If they failed and the enemy overran their position the rest of the battalion would not have enough time to come to their aid and more than likely they would be in a dire predicament themselves. For the past two weeks the enemy, not three hundred yards in front of them, had shelled them, harassing fire coming in at all times of day and night, snipers making everyone keep their heads low during the day.

It was a clear night, the silvery light of the moon and the million stars shining in the sky bathing the landscape with a ghost-like glow. Andrew drew on his cigarette, his hands cupped over it in order not to show the glow of the tip and released the smoke slowly, savoring the tobacco. Every day he made the decision to stop smoking and every day he broke it. The damn thing is taking hold of me; Andrew stood up and stretched his body, yawning. He was tired, but not sleepy and looking at his watch he realized that his guard duty was almost over. Another thirty minutes and he would be able to lie down. The post was more of a listening post than anything else, but on this particular night with the moon and the stars visibility was good. He felt something wet touch his face and he looked up. Snowflakes were coming down, big ones, sticking to the frozen earth, covering it rapidly. Andrew shuddered in his field jacket, his eyes straining to see what lay in front of him. He heard footsteps to his rear, approaching slowly and he came immediately to attention, wondering who it could be. He waited and eventually a shadow detached itself from the night and Paul J. Ragsdale walked to him, two mugs of steaming coffee in his hands, his rifle slung over one shoulder.

"Thought you might like something hot," he said, handing one of the canteen cups to Andrew, his voice no more than a whisper. On a night like this Andrew had told him noise would go a long way and he sure as hell didn't want to attract the attention of the bad boys across from them. They sat together, talking quietly, their eyes glued to the terrain in front of them.

"Man it's cold," Ragsdale said, sucking on the canteen cup, the coffee cooling rapidly.

"Yes, it…" Andrew said, cutting himself off suddenly, coming to his feet in one fluid motion, the coffee spilling from his hand. He heard the whistling noise cutting the air and he immediately knew what it was. He barely had time for one warning yell when the mortar round landed, exploding to their immediate left, fragments ricocheting from the rocks. Both men whirled around and ran for their lives while all around them the night was rendered with the sounds of explosion, mortar rounds coming over their heads. They reached the trench line and dove into it, listening to the sound of men running, the explosions coming one after the other in rapid succession. They crouched in the trench making themselves as small as possible while dirt and rocks flew all over them. For what seemed like an eternity, but was no longer than a few minutes, the bombardment continued and as suddenly as it had started it stopped. For a few seconds Andrew remained on the ground smelling the dirt in front of his face, listening to the wild staccato that was his heart. An eerie silence followed the bombardment and then Andrew Beck got up, sneaking a peek over the trench. Seeing nothing he rolled over the edge, crawling a few yards to a rock outcropping.

"Where the hell are you going," Ragsdale asked, seeing his friend disappear over the edge of the trench. He didn't get an answer and he followed suit, wondering what Andrew was doing. Reaching his friend he got up. He started to say something when he felt Andrew's hand grabbing him, his fingers like steel claws digging into his arm. Andrew was standing still, his body hidden by the rock outcropping, looking ahead.

"What the…" he started, but never finished, his eyes fixed on the slopes two hundred yards from them.

And then his blood froze in his veins. At first he thought that the moonlight was playing tricks on him. He could swear that the whole slope was moving and then he realized that what he was looking at was a mass of humanity walking toward their emplacement. At that moment the whole mass seemed to explode, the figures running and a tremendous yell reverberated across the stillness of the night.

"Run, Paul, Run," he heard Andrew yelling, the sound of the M-1 firing loud in his ears. At that moment, firing erupted all over the front line as more and more GIs on guard realized what was coming. Once again they took off, searching for the safety of the bunkers, while a human avalanche rolled after them, fanatical screams sending shivers down their spine.

Reaching the trench they yelled at the top of their lungs, fearing that one of their own would shoot them down in their terror. By the time they were safely inside the trenches, bullets were flying everywhere, the sound of artillery rounds and mortars screaming in the night. Pandemonium broke out and Andrew looked around, seeing the fear and terror etched deeply in the faces around him. He saw Sgt. Walker running followed closely by Captain Cherry, heading for the trenches and then he was busy firing at the shadows in front of them. Hand grenades started coming in, the explosions bouncing them up in the air, the noise deafening, their ears ringing. Andrew emptied his rifle at the forms trying to come over the bunker, listening to the screams of men wounded and dying. Men fell to the right and left of him until it was just he and Paul and several more men in the trench. Snapping another magazine into his rifle he looked around, seeing Captain Cherry come over the edge of the trench, Walker right behind him. At that moment a grenade came sailing in, bouncing off Andrew's helmet. Without thinking, Andrew reached for it, throwing it back at the red tide threatening to overwhelm them. The grenade went off, but it was so close that fragments peppered the trench, one piece hitting Andrew a glancing blow to the head, blood flowing down his face. He shook his head to dispel the pain and continued to fire at the enemy. He looked around one more time, just in time to see Captain Cherry go down, a bullet through his mouth, another hitting him on his chest. The man tumbled, his legs folding on him like wheat felled by a giant knife blade. He ran to him, mindless of his own wound, and yelled for a medic. Without waiting he applied his own first aid pouch to the wound, wrapping it as best he could. The noise around them was infernal, the smell of cordite and blood permeated the air, the sound of fifty caliber machine guns a constant in the night. Flares had finally gone up, illuminating the battle and here and there he could see men engaged in hand-to-hand combat. Despite the cold he was sweating, the blood from his head wound mixing with it, getting in his mouth and eyes. Running back to the edge of the trench he joined Paul, emptying his rifle again. He was in the process of reloading when a figure came over the edge, followed rapidly by two more. With a guttural sound escaping his lips, Andrew jumped, reversing his rifle and hitting the Korean on the face with the butt, the man's face disintegrating in a splash of red. He looked around to see Sgt. Walker and Paul engaged in hand-to-hand combat with the two other soldiers and he rushed to help. Before he was able to reach Walker the Korean soldier gained the upper hand and swiftly, put a bayonet into him, pinning him to the ground. With an animal scream, Andrew charged the Korean, his rifle smashing against the man's skull, over and over until the rifle broke in two and the man toppled over, crashing to the ground. Whirling around, Andrew searched frantically for a weapon, his eyes taking in the fight all around him. In the dancing light of the illuminating flares he could see that the red tide had been able to breach the trenches and with a look of desperation on his face, Andrew realized that only a few of them were alive. Without preamble he rejoined the fight, snatching a BAR (Browning Automatic Rifle) from the ground and a bandoleer full of magazines for it. Searching for Paul he found him under a dead enemy, blood pouring out of him from a shoulder wound. One more time he crouched low, looking frantically for a first aid pouch, finding one and stuffing it on the wound. He could feel his friend breathing raggedly but strong and he said a silent prayer. Snatching his BAR he ran to the edge of the trench, rolled over and came to his feet. He felt light-headed, the adrenaline coursing through his body making everything crystal clear. He looked down in the trench and saw a group of GIs cowering at the bottom, their rifles thrown on the ground. To hell with this, he thought, I'm not about to die in this trench like a rat. A look of pure rage and determination was etched on his young face and with a last look around he charged the incoming enemy, yelling at the remaining GIs in the trenches. "Come on, damn it, come on," he said, his face a snarl of agony, his eyes haunted. He felt bullets grazing his clothes, like angry bees they buzzed his head and he ran a zigzag pattern. The BAR jumped in his hand as he fired, men falling all around him, their screams reverberating in the night. Observing the enemy silhouetted against the skyline he rushed them. A tremendous blow to his right leg knocked him to the ground and he realized he had been shot. Grimacing he stood up, the pain coursing through him like wildfire, making him nauseous. Ignoring the pain he closed again with the enemy, emptying the BAR, reloading and firing again, until it finally clicked empty and he was out of ammo. Snatching another rifle from the ground he knocked soldiers right and left, the bayonet slicing into men's stomachs, blood splashing on him. From behind him, he heard firing and turned around to see the few GIs that were left, following him. How long the fight lasted he didn't know, but eventually his brain told him that silence had come. In a daze he looked around, his eyes registering the incredible devastation surrounding him. Dead bodies were everywhere, blood staining the fresh snow. He walked around, ignoring his own wounds, checking the bodies of the fallen GIs. With the help of the few GIs left he helped the wounded ones, making a makeshift first-aid station in a bunker. He came to where Paul was and found him semiconscious, breathing steadily. He checked his wound one more time, noticing that the cold had slowed down the bleeding. He reached for a blanket and tenderly wrapped his friend in it. Summoning another soldier, they transported him to the makeshift hospital. Andrew looked around attempting to find an officer, only to realize that none were left. Remembering Captain Cherry he came to where he had seen the man go down and found him sitting against the side of the trench, blood covering his face and chest. A bullet had gone through his mouth, knocking out teeth and exiting through his cheek, smashing his jawbone, another hitting him on the chest. The man was alive, but in incredible pain and Andrew helped him up, supporting him, walking carefully to the bunker.

They needed medical help and soon or most of these fellows would die. He looked around noticing some of the survivors milling around, most of them in a daze. He called in a strong voice and several of them came to him. They were filthy and some of them had superficial wounds but nothing that would prevent them from a little work. He looked at his own leg, blood still dripping from his wound and he ripped the pant leg open. A small hole could be seen in his right thigh, blood and watery fluids seeping slowly from it. The flesh around the hole was purple-black and with his fingers he attempted to locate an exit hole. He could feel a bullet just about to break the skin, but there was no exit. He wrapped the leg as best he could and continued to hobble around.

"I'm PFC Beck," he said, digging in his pocket and fishing out a cigarette from a crumpled pack, lighting one and passing the rest around. "I need somebody to go to the CP(Command Post) and see if we can get communication restored with Battalion headquarters. I'm pretty sure they know what the situation is, but we need to tell them about our wounded and that we need medical help." He paused for a second, his mind searching. They needed so many things, he thought, knowing that it would be a while before help would come their way. If this had been an all out offensive, then the whole front would be in need of replacement and medics. They would just have to wait their turn.

One or two guys raised their hands, their eyes vacant and Andrew dispatched them to see about the communications. "The rest of you guys get busy, help the wounded, do whatever needs to be done." He took a deep drag of the cigarette and threw it down, crushing it. "Now, let's go," he said, dismissing the men, walking around until he found a serviceable rifle and enough ammo. He walked to the same place where he had been standing when the fight started, sat on top of the bunker and resumed his vigilance of the front. Sometime while he was busy, daylight had come, a watery sun in an overcast sky attempting to show its face. It had stopped snowing, the ground covered with it, but not enough to cover the incredible devastation that had taken place just a few hours ago. Andrew looked around at the hundreds of dead bodies littering the slopes of the hill and he marveled at the fact that he wasn't one of them.

He sat still for a while, a cigarette dangling from the corner of his mouth, the smoke drifting up. He was immersed in his thoughts when he heard footsteps approaching and he looked up briefly.

Lt. Colonel Devlin walked to his side and stopped, a frown etched deeply on his forehead.

"My God," he said, his voice husky, his eyes taking in the terrain and the terrible fight that had taken place there, seeing the bodies of the enemy strewn all over the place, blood covering the pristine snow, "what the hell happened here?"

He looked at the young man expectantly, but the man didn't move or answer and that annoyed him. Colonel Devlin was a career officer, a West Point man and a veteran of World War II. He fixed his eyes on the man, sitting on top of the bunker and he saw a smile flicker across his young face. And then the man spoke, a strong, pleasant voice with a Texas accent.

"We kicked their butts good," he said, flicking ashes on the ground. And then the man turned around to face him and Colonel Devlin saw his face. As accustomed as he thought he was to death and wounds, Colonel Devlin gasped at the sight of the young man's face. His whole left side was covered with dry and fresh blood running down on his chest. His clothes were filthy and his right leg was also covered with blood. Looking closely Colonel Devlin was able to see that the young man had been wounded several times. How the man was still on his feet was beyond him and he reached a hand to him.

"You are wounded, son," he said, his voice gentle now.

"Yes, I am…", he said noncommittally and then, looking at the silver leaf on the officer's shoulder he said, "Sir." He struggled to get up, almost falling in the process. While sitting down his leg had stiffened and he would have fallen if not for the strong hand of colonel Devlin assisting him.

"I'm all right," he said, his mind dealing with the pain, relegating it to the back of his mind. This time he omitted the sir, but Devlin didn't rebuke him.

"Who is in charge here?" he asked, looking around.

"I guess I am, Sir," Andrew answered, hobbling on one good leg. "Captain Cherry was wounded at the beginning of the fight," he continued, taking small steps. "I believe I am the ranking man." He stopped walking and turned toward the Colonel, dropping the cigarette and standing at attention.

"I'm PFC Beck, Sir," he said, his hand coming up and rendering a parade perfect salute to a superior officer. Devlin looked at him, not expecting that now and saw the pain reflected on the young man's eyes. He was at the end of his rope, exhausted, but he would continue until his duty was done.

Colonel Devlin saluted back, moisture filling his eyes and he looked at the young man in front of him with interest. All around them was activity and Andrew could see new faces manning the bunkers and the trenches.

"You better tell me what happened here, Lieutenant," he said, "and then we will see about your wounds."

"You got it wrong, Sir," he said. "It's Private Beck, Sir."

"Not any more," Colonel Devlin said. "From now own you are a second Lieutenant. You just earned a field promotion."

Andrew thought about that for a few seconds and a tired smile came to his face. Well what about that, an officer, he thought, thinking that his father would really be proud of him now. Colonel Devlin saw the look in the young man's face and he laughed.

"Congratulations, Lieutenant," he said. They stopped at the entrance of the makeshift hospital, Andrew seeing GIs coming back and forth, transporting wounded men into ambulances. The next man coming out was Captain Cherry and they stood aside to let them pass. He was awake, his eyes reflecting the pain. Seeing the Colonel he signaled the bearers to stop. He tried to raise himself on one elbow, but the effort was too much. He lay back down, his eyes fixed on Andrew and he attempted to say something. Once again it was impossible to do it and he gave up, the bandages across his face preventing him from talking. For a moment his eyes locked on Andrew's face trying to convey whatever it was he wanted to say. He nodded his head and then they were gone. Walking inside Andrew noticed someone had rigged a light and several medics were working on the most serious cases. He looked for Paul and found him resting quietly in a corner. He had been tagged by a medic and was awaiting transportation.

He was awake now, the eternal cigarette in his mouth. "How are you?" he asked, bending over his friend.

"I'm fine, cowboy," Paul answered. "Just a small bullet hole in my shoulder. Medic said I will be okay in a couple of weeks, maybe three." He paused for a second, readjusting himself on the narrow stretcher. "And what about you?" he asked, his eyes looking him over.

"I'm fine Paul, just fine," he said, the grimace on his face making him a liar.

"Just a nick here and there, but I'll be okay." At that time the medics came for Paul and Andrew got up, hobbling again. The medics looked at Paul and then one on each end lifted the stretcher, preparing to go.

"Take care my friend," Andrew said, his hand squeezing his arm. He found himself a place to sit and saw Colonel Devlin talking with another officer, a silver-haired man with large, intelligent eyes. The Colonel looked over at Andrew and said a few more words to the other man and then he came over, bending down to talk to him. Before he had a chance to say anything, a short barrel-chested man approached them, coming to at ease. Andrew noticed the Sgt. Major rank on the collar, an E-9, probably the Battalion Command Sgt. Major, Andrew thought, looking at the man. He noticed the nametag, Moran, and the large cigar in the corner of his mouth. Colonel Devlin looked up and his eyebrow rose in a silent question.

"Able and Baker Companies have been decimated, Sir," Moran said, consulting a small notebook in his hand. "Of a compliment of 89 men there are thirteen left, including him," he said, his head indicating Andrew. He took a drag of the cigar and then continued. "It's the same story all over the line, except that it appears that the brunt of the fight was in front of Able Company. We found more than two hundred enemy dead, Sir, an incredible number of them by butt stroke or bayonet." He stopped, waiting for the Colonel to speak. Devlin nodded his head in acknowledgment, his brow creased in thought.

"Get Echo Company up here, Sgt. Major," he said. "Make sure they are informed of what happened and that they are now the forward unit in this section. Notify division headquarters also."

Sgt. Major Moran nodded his head, all the time scribbling furiously on the note pad. When he finished he looked at the Colonel expectantly. Devlin looked around, finding the man he had talked to before and signaled him forward. When the man reached them Andrew could see a major's leaves on one side of his collar and the insignia of the medical corps on the other. Devlin nodded his head and the man bent down toward Andrew.

"This is Major Brady, son," he said. "The Battalion surgeon. He will take care of you while we talk."

"Just lie still," Major Brady said, starting to cut Andrew's pants away from his leg.

"Sgt. Major, you take notes," Devlin said, "while Lt. Beck here tells us what happened."

While the surgeon probed and checked all over his body Andrew tried his best to tell Colonel Devlin what had transpired just a few hours ago, the Sgt. Major stopping him every once in a while for clarification on something. When he was done there was silence for a while and then Lt. Colonel Devlin spoke.

"You did a great job up here son," he said, his voice full of emotion. He had been a soldier all his life and from the beginning had known that the young man lying on the stretcher had a lot to do with the fact that they had not been overrun and completely exterminated. "I'll make sure that you all are rewarded for your actions."

Andrew looked at the Colonel closely and then he said, "It was a team effort, Sir, and besides that, I was just doing my duty."

Colonel Devlin heard the young man's words and he shook his head. The boy was modest too, he thought, I will definitely put him up for the Medal of Honor. He got up, signaling the end of the interview and he nodded his head to the Major.

The doctor injected him with something and in a few minutes his head rolled to the side and he was out, his breathing normal.

"Got everything?" he asked, looking at the Sgt. Major.

"Yes, Sir," Moran said, putting his notes away. "I'll go and talk with some of the others and have this typed later Colonel." Saying that he came briefly to attention and turned around, exiting the bunker.

Major Brady called a pair of medics over and pointed at Andrew. "Have him transported to the nearest MASH unit as soon as possible," he said, turning around to face Devlin.

"He will be fine, Colonel. He lost a lot of blood from that leg wound and the head, but he should recover nicely. He is young and strong and he will be back in no time."

Devlin thanked him, letting the man return to his duties and then he walked outside. He ran his hand through his short hair and his mind returned to the task at hand. With a deep sigh he looked around, finding the Sgt. Major sitting in his jeep.

"Let's go, Moran," he said, walking toward the front lines. "We have a lot of work to do and I don't want to get caught with our pants down again.

# 13

U.S. Army, Pusan, South Korea
4027th MASH Unit
25 November 1950

The first time Andrew Beck woke up it was to a world of pain and confusion. Just barely conscious he tried to raise his head and stars formed in front of his eyes. He fell back on the bed, weak and nauseous. The world spun again and he drifted, his eyes closing.

The next time it was slightly better, the pain not as bad. He lay still, his mind confused. He opened his eyes slowly, or at least his left eye. Something was covering the right side of his face and he raised his hand, touching it tenderly. He closed his eye again, the pain in his head like something eating him alive. His mind cleared and he remembered the bloody battle and that he had been wounded. And then, slowly he took inventory of the rest of his body. His right leg was rigged to something, cables holding it still, while he was sure a bandage was on his head. I must be in some kind of hospital, he thought, looking around with his good eye. He was in an army tent and he could see other GIs next to him. He could also hear the sound of people talking and he relaxed, waiting for someone to come. He needed some water, his mouth was parched and he could hardly swallow. He didn't have long to wait before he heard the sound of a woman's voice next to him and realized that it was a nurse talking to the patient next to him. She finished talking to the soldier and then turned around facing Andrew. Her eyes registered surprise when she saw his eye open and a smile came to her face.

"Well," she said coming to stand by his bed, a cool hand touching his forehead. "I see you have decided to come back to the world of the living."

Andrew tried to talk but only managed a croaked sound. He tried again, his throat contracting at the effort. He looked at the nurse and she smiled at him again. "Wait a second," she said, disappearing from sight only to come back moments later with a cup in her hand. "Drink this," she said helping him to raise his head.

He managed a few swallows and then had to drop his head again, the world swimming in front of his eyes.

"Where… where am I?" he asked, his voice weak.

"You are in a MASH unit," she said, leaning toward him. "You have been here three days." She had short brown hair, he noticed, and freckles on her face. She rearranged his bed, fussing over him and then she was gone, telling him that the doctor would be coming by to see him shortly.

He drifted back to sleep until a hand on his shoulder woke him up. This time there were no stars in front of his eyes, but his head still felt like someone had used it for baseball practice.

He focused his eye on the person who had awakened him and saw a ruddy-faced man, the gold leaf of a major on his shirt collar, leaning over him. He looked at the name on the tag—Wilson. The man had strong but gentle hands and he talked softly while he worked over Andrew. He probed and pinched, checking the head and the leg, his chest and his heart and when he was satisfied he stopped. Consulting a chart in his hand he looked at Andrew.

"You have been here three days son," he said, his pale blue eyes fixed on Andrew, " and I'm a little worried about your leg. I'm afraid we have to send you to Japan and possibly the States." He saw the look that came to Andrew's face and he hurried to allay his fears. "Nothing to worry about Lieutenant," he said, "just a precaution. We want to be sure the leg is going to be all right." The doctor bent over him again, his hands moving over his face, removing the bandages slowly.

"You are lucky the shrapnel didn't come any closer to your eye," Dr. Wilson said, checking the wound. The hot metal had cut a furrow in his scalp beginning just above his eyebrow, slicing through his flesh like hot butter and finally taking a small piece of his ear off.

"That is healing nicely," Dr. Wilson said, finishing his examination. "You will be leaving today for Japan and I'm recommending that you go to Walter Reed to have that leg worked on. Any questions?"

"No, nothing that I can think of, Sir," he said. He didn't feel like talking, just wanted to be left alone. Dr. Wilson nodded his head and turned around to leave. He had taken a couple of steps when he stopped, whirling around to face Andrew one more time.

"Damn, I forgot this," he said, his hand going to his pocket, searching for something. He finally found what he was looking for, his hand coming out with a small case. Handing it to Andrew he said, "A Colonel Devlin came by a couple of days ago and left this for you."

Andrew reached for the case, wondering what it was. He opened the case slowly, his eyes taking in the contents of the case. Inside, nestled in purple cloth was a medal, purple cloth on top and the medal in the shape of a heart, the head of President George Washington embedded in it. The Purple Heart, Andrew thought, his mind going back to the first one he had ever seen, his father's.

"Thank you, Sir," he said softly, closing the lid.

Dr. Wilson nodded his head one more time and then he said, "he also wanted me to tell you that he will see that a copy of the citation that goes with that is put on your 201 file, also a copy of your promotion to Second Lieutenant." Andrew said a feeble thank you again and finally the Major departed, leaving Andrew with his thoughts. A short time later two medics came to get him ready for the plane ride to Japan and within minutes he was on his way along with several other GIs. Once aboard the plane a nurse came by giving him a shot of something and within minutes he was asleep.

He woke up in another hospital, this time in Japan where he was poked and examined again by a doctor and the next morning he was on his way again, this time for the United States. When a nurse showed up with the needle just after departure he refused to take it.

"I don't want that, mam," he said, eyeing the needle like it was an enemy. He was tired of drifting away into sleep, tired of needles and drugs. "I would rather be awake and go to sleep on my own than take any more of those shots."

The nurse looked at him for a few seconds and then she shook her head, putting the hypodermic needle away.

"How is the pain?" she asked, looking at his chart and making notations.

"I can take it," Andrew said, his face now expressionless. I will be damned if I tell this woman how much it hurts, he thought, especially the leg.

"Well, if you change your mind let me know," she said, giving him a look that said she didn't believe him at all.

Andrew saw her go and a smile flickered across his face. He ran his hand over his face, feeling the roughness of his three or four day growth of beard, his hand touching the bandages on his head. There was hardly any pain to that wound, but when he moved his hand to his leg it was different. The pain was still there, sometimes just a throb and sometimes sharp, but there nonetheless. The hours passed slowly on the plane and finally he succumbed to sleep, the monotonous drone of the propellers serving as balm to his tired nerves.

# 14

U.S. Army
Walter Reed Hospital
Washington, DC
14 December 1950

Andrew Beck walked slowly down an immaculate corridor of the hospital, a cane assisting him while at his side a nurse evaluated his progress. He had arrived at the hospital several days ago and was looking forward to being discharged.

According to the doctors they had been able to repair the damage to the leg and there was no reason why he couldn't recuperate fully. At first there had been some doubt that he would be able to walk normally, but they were not counting on Andrew's will and determination. When he was told, he grilled the doctors asking all kinds of questions, eager to find out everything possible concerning his leg. He was told that there would be an operation and then it would be up to him to exercise the leg and do physical therapy. He had done that with the same vigor and grim determination that he did everything else and it had paid off. His leg was almost back to normal.

Finishing his walk he returned to his bed, picking up a book that he had been reading. He had spent most of his time at the hospital in a state of complete boredom until one of the nurses suggested reading. He had never been very fond of that but with no place to go and the hours drifting slowly by, Andrew gave up his reticence and started reading. It wasn't long before he realized that he really enjoyed it and the nurses started bringing new material and books to him. The one in his hand was a book of poetry by a man named T. H. Lawrence and he found that it was his favorite type of reading. He read a few lines of a new poem and then gave a deep sigh and put the book down.

His mind had been going full tilt lately concerning Catherine and the fact that he had not received any letters from her. He had written several times and by now she should have gotten them. He had started writing from Korea and now several letters since he had been at the hospital in Washington. And he heard nothing from her. He shook his head to dispel the bad thoughts and decided that there must be a reason why she had not written or answered any of his letters. She could be sick, he thought, or something happened.

He was deep in his thoughts when he noticed a man standing by his bed, a brief case in his hand.

The man was dressed in class "A" uniform and he could see the railroad tracks of a Captain on his shoulders. He was young with a round face and small eyes behind gold-rimmed glasses.

Paper pusher, Andrew thought, his eyes going over the man. And then the officer spoke, his voice small and squeaky.

"Lieutenant Beck?" he asked, making it more of a fact than a question.

Andrew fixed his eyes on him and nodded his head in response. Just what he needed, another paper pusher with bad news, he thought, wondering what the man was all about.

The Captain approached the bed, opening his case and taking out several papers. "I'm Captain Richardson from personnel," he said, arranging the papers on the bed to his satisfaction. "The doctors are about to release you from the hospital and they have advised us so I thought I could come here and save you a trip to the Pentagon." He looked carefully at the papers and picked one, handing it to Andrew.

"That is your copy of the orders making you a Second Lieutenant," he said and then picking another paper and doing the same again. "This one is your authorization to allow you to wear a CIB (Combat Infantry Badge) and the Purple Heart and this one is your leave papers allowing you thirty days before you have to report back for duty." He paused for a minute his hands busy with more papers.

"This is your pay voucher and a check," he said pushing more papers in front of Andrew. "Sign here," he said, a pudgy finger showing him where. He stopped talking long enough to scribble something on a piece of paper, handing it to him.

"Notify us at this number where you will be as soon as you are settled in. Any Questions?" he asked.

"No... No questions, but I don't want to go on leave, Captain," he said, thinking that there was no place he wanted to go, no family, just Catherine and he was beginning to have a bad feeling about that. "I need to go back to my unit." Captain Richardson looked at him with what Andrew thought was a know-it-all look, snapping his briefcase closed.

"You have your orders Lieutenant," he said. "When the Army thinks you are ready for duty they will let you know." He nodded his head briefly waiting a few more seconds and then left Andrew alone.

A couple of hours later the doctor came by and after checking the leg one more time had signed his discharge paper, only to find out that he didn't have any civilian or military clothes with him. His nurse solved that problem, taking his measurements and going out on her lunch hour to buy him clothes. Andrew was touched by her gesture and thanked her profusely.

She had done well, Andrew thought, looking at himself in the bathroom mirror. She had bought a gray suit, a white shirt, a tie, underwear, socks and shoes and even if the clothes were inexpensive they looked good on him. He was thinner and his face was pale. He looked at himself again, closer this time, noticing the red angry scar on the right side of his head, almost covered by his hair and then he noticed something in his eyes that had not been there before. Sadness, he thought, that's what it is. He had gone into the lair of death and had conquered his fears, but it had cost him and he had paid the price. No longer was he the same idealistic young man who had cheerfully volunteered, no longer the green recruit. He had been tested and found that he had in him what was needed to do the job. He also found out that there was no glory in war, just pain and suffering and death and that the most sacred duty of a soldier would be to fight for peace.

It was a changed Andrew Beck who walked out of Walter Reed Hospital on a cold day in December, a young man determined to do his job to the best of his abilities, guided by the power of God and the dictates of his conscience.

# 15

Washington, DC
16 December 1950

It was cold in Washington and Andrew walked rapidly down the street, his hands jammed in his pockets. He had been thinking about what to do with his time, finally admitting to himself that he wanted to find out about Catherine. He had the address now all he needed was the courage to go and see her. He loved her, he knew that, but his mind kept coming back to the fact that they were from different worlds. He thought about the possibility that she had been lying to him, that she didn't love him at all and had only been playing with him, but immediately regretted thinking that, his mind going back to the nights they had spent together in the motel room. He had made up his mind and was now on his way to the train station. He bought a ticket and shortly afterwards was on his way to Boston. It was a long trip and he slept most of the way, his body still suffering from the affect of his wounds. He noticed that the cold made his leg hurt and he had to massage the wound in order for it to feel better.

Brooklyne, Boston
16 December 1950

It was snowing when he arrived in Boston, the sky almost black despite the fact that it was still daylight and he shuddered in his thin suit. He had not gotten an overcoat and decided to fix that as soon as he could. He hailed a taxi finding out that it would cost him twenty dollars to reach the address. A look from the driver told him clearly that he didn't belong in that neighborhood.

Thirty minutes later he was in front of a magnificent house, bigger than anything Andrew had ever seen before and his heart beat loudly in his ears. As befitting such a place and the status of the owners, it was decorated for the season, Christmas lights and red ribbons in every tree and bush surrounding the house. An enormous wreath beautifully decorated could be seen on the door, smaller ones on every window in the place. Even the fences that surrounded the yard were festooned with decorations, giving the place a festive look. He got out of the taxi and looked at the imposing building, mustering the courage to go up and knock on the door. It's funny, he thought, I can face death with a smile on my face, but I can hardly walk up to that door.

"Wait here," he said, exiting the car.

He shook his head ruefully and then with his mind made up he walked to the door and knocked loudly. He waited a few moments and was about to knock again when the door opened and a tall, black man stood in front of him. He looked at Andrew with large inquisitive eyes and then he said, "Yes sir, may I help you?"

Andrew looked at the man for a few seconds and then he stammered. "I… I would like to see Miss Weatherly," he said. "Catherine Weatherly."

"And whom may I say is calling, sir?" he asked, his eyes taking in the inexpensive clothes and the fact that the young man was shivering without an overcoat.

"I'm Andrew Beck," he said and he could swear that something came into the man's eyes at the mention of his name.

For a long moment the black man didn't answer him, a deep frown on his face and then his features softened and a look of pity came into his eyes.

"Miss Weatherly is not home, sir," he said, his voice soft, almost a whisper. "She is in Europe, on her…" he cut himself off, something like tears coming into his eyes and then clearing his throat he continued, "on her honeymoon."

For a moment Andrew thought he had heard wrong and he just looked at the man, his brain finally absorbing what he had heard.

"Honeymoon? What honeymoon?" he asked, his voice loud now, confusion etched on his handsome face. "What the hell are you talking about?"

He saw the Negro man look over his shoulder like he was fearful someone might hear them talking and then the man took a step toward him, his eyes sad.

"Miss Weatherly was married last week, Sir," he said, "and…" once again he cut himself off, clamping his mouth shut like a man who had said too much.

"Married? That's impossible," Andrew said, his mind a whirlwind of emotions. What the hell had happened to Catherine, to all her promises, he thought, his head feeling like it was going to split. He stood there like a man who had just received a death sentence, his brain reeling at the import of what he had just heard.

He shivered feeling numb and then he squared his shoulders, breathed deeply, and regained his composure. He fixed his eyes on the man in front of him and for a second he thought the black man was going to say something else, but he must have thought better of it and decided not to.

Dejected, Andrew walked back to the taxi, confused and angry at what he thought was a betrayal by the woman that he loved. He climbed back in the car, his eyes dark and smoldering, feeling the cold rage engulfing his entire being.

"Let's go," he said and the taxi driver drove off.

From the entrance to the house Benjamin saw him go, his heart aching for the young man and for Miss Weatherly. Silently he closed the door, his feet heavy, and feeling like he was a hundred years old.

# 16

Stonewall, Texas
25 December 1950

    Andrew Beck sat next to the wood burning stove in his old shack, feeding it small pieces of wood, and getting the fire going good. The place was cold in winter and the stove burned an incredible amount of wood, forcing him to cut and stack wood for most of the day. He sat there for a while listening to the crackling of the wood as it burned, his mind on Catherine, making him wonder how he had been such a fool. He had departed from her house, his brain reeling at the words of the black man. He loved Catherine and he could swear that she loved him too, and now his whole world had been turned upside down. He had gone back to the bus station, returning to Stonewall, unwilling to let anyone see his pain. He had gone and seen the Fitzgeralds, taking the opportunity to call the number that he was given and letting them know where he would be and then saying his goodbye he had gone to the old shack, making it livable again. He spent the first few days taking it easy, resting his leg and then on the third day had gone hunting, testing the leg. He had spent most of the day outside, the wind and the cold his constant companions until he was famished and with his leg throbbing he had returned to the shack. He cooked some meat and beans and after eating he sat drinking coffee. He was pleased with himself and the way his leg had performed during the day. He had bagged a fairly good size deer and he realized that he hadn't lost any of his old hunting skills. He kept to himself, reading and thinking, becoming one with the land again until the cabin got to be too much and he needed to get out. He had borrowed a horse from the Fitzgerald's but didn't relish the thought of going to Stonewall on Christmas day on a horse so he had tinkered with his father's old Ford pick-up truck behind the shed until finally the motor sputtered and caught, running rough but steady.

He made his way to town finding the old Mexican cantina almost deserted and proceeded to get drunk, slowly and methodically and for the first time in his life. He knew he was feeling sorry for himself, but he couldn't care less right now. All he wanted to do was to drink enough whisky to deaden the pain.

How he ever made it home he never knew, but the next day he woke up with an incredible headache, the world spinning crazily. He nursed his first hangover for a day and then he went out again, hunting the elusive game around the Lazy B ranch until he grew tired and restless of that too and decided it was time to get back. New Year had come and gone and it was getting close to the time he was supposed to report back. His country was fighting a war and he didn't need to stay out of it any longer. His leg had mended well and he decided to call that number a few days ahead of time and see if he could get back in the war.

Early the next morning after a cup of black coffee and a cigarette he got in his old pick-up truck and after several tries had it running, backfiring and sputtering all the way. He made his way to the Fitzgerald's house, arriving early enough to share breakfast with them. Emma and Stanley Fitzgerald were just like family to him and in a way he almost felt at home in their modest house. Stanley saw him coming and walked out on the porch, waiting for him. He was a tall, skinny man tough as rawhide, but getting old, and the weather-beaten face showing a lifetime of hard work.

"I'm glad you are here, son," he said, opening the door for him, stepping right behind him. The heat of the house hit Andrew as he walked through the door making him realized how cold it was outside. "Some fellow from the Army had called here twice in the past two days, wanting to talk with you, said it was important." They went into the kitchen, the smell of bacon and eggs permeating the air. Stanley handed Andrew a cup of coffee and they sat down at the table, Emma bringing the food.

He ate with gusto, the fresh air and the cold awakening his appetite. After he finished he fished for the number given and sat down to make the call. He got a response on the first ring. He had found out the first time he called that he was calling Fort Myer and wondered what was going on. He gave his name and rank to the person at the other end of the line and then someone else came on.

"Lieutenant Beck?" the voice asked.

"Yes, Sir," Andrew said.

"I'm Colonel Miller, Public Relations Officer for Ft. Myer," he said, pausing for a second and then continuing. "You are to report to me by VOCG (verbal order of Commanding General) at Ft. Myer within three days. Once you get here we will make further arrangements for your stay and will give you further orders. Any questions?"

"Yes, Sir, if I may ask," he said, "What is going on?"

He heard a chuckle at the other end of the line and then Colonel Miller said, "You are getting a medal son." He hung up after that, leaving Andrew confused. He thought about the conversation for a minute and then shrugged his shoulders. He would find out more when he got there, he thought. He said his goodbye again and made the trip home. Once there he packed his few belongings, turned the horse loose and locked the door to the rambling shack. He looked around the lonely place one more time, the setting sun casting a world full of shadows on the land. He got in the pick-up truck and made his way back to Stonewall. He had made arrangements with Stanley to pick up the truck in the morning and there was nothing else that needed to be done. In the bus station he bought his ticket and sat down to wait, the bus finally showing up fifteen minutes late. He got in, found a seat to himself in the half empty bus and within minutes was fast asleep.

# 17

Fort Myer, Virginia
11 January 1951
1400 hours

He arrived in Ft. Myer almost broke after three days on the road. Getting a taxi from the bus station to the post was going to be a problem, Andrew thought, knowing that he was almost penniless. He was debating what to do when he saw the sign on the bus counter.

Ft. Myer arrivals, Officers call 319-3465, ext. 419
Enlisted call 319-4579, ext. 319

There was a phone next to the sign and he approached calling the number. When he got an answer he was asked several questions and he gave his rank and name and was told that there would be a jeep to pick him up within thirty minutes. He hung up and wandered around for a few minutes, watching the hustle and bustle of the station. When he returned to the counter it was to find a Staff Sergeant (E-6) waiting for him. Andrew approached him and after ascertaining that the Sergeant was there for him they made their way out, arriving on post in a matter of minutes. Andrew looked at the view realizing that the post was well maintained, everything freshly painted and clean. This was the home of the Honor Guards and Arlington Cemetery and he presumed they had just about the best of everything.

The jeep deposited him in front of an old building, the sign outside proclaiming it to be the Office of Public Relations and he got out, walking the few steps to the door and going in. Once inside he looked around and was greeted by a soft female voice, a young woman sitting at a desk to his left, a small tag proclaiming that she was Miss Talbot.

"May I help you sir," she asked and Andrew faced her. It was a receptionist and after he gave her his name she consulted a list and announced that Colonel Miller was waiting for him. She picked up the phone and said a few words, hanging up almost immediately. She was young with long black hair framing her face. Her eyes were almost lavender, bright and inquisitive.

"The Colonel will be out in a few minutes, Lieutenant," she said, her glance taking in the tall Texan. He was young, she thought, not much older than she was and wondered how he could have done all the things that the citation said he had. But once she looked into his eyes, a shudder went through her and something told her that the man in front of her was capable of what they said and more. There was a look of quiet assurance in the man, the way he stood while he waited, ramrod straight and the way he looked and then, there were those eyes, a grayish-green that she knew could freeze your soul and she thought again that, yes, the man was dangerous. But when he looked at her she saw his face change, something like an infinite sadness clouded his eyes and even though he smiled she could see the pain reflected in them. It was the look of a man much older, a man who had seen death and suffering and had been tempered by it. She felt like reaching out to him, to touch his face and place his head on her breast, the feelings so strong that she blushed, a hollow sensation in the pit of her stomach. Andrew was aware of the looks that the woman was giving him, and he fidgeted, wishing that the

Colonel would come on and explain to him what he was doing here. He cleared his throat and was about to say something when a door opened at the end of the corridor and a man of medium height, wearing a silver leaf, the rank of a Lieutenant Colonel, made his way toward him.

Andrew was in civilian clothes but he still came to attention. The Colonel approached him with a smile on his face.

"I'm Lieutenant Andrew Beck, Sir," he said, "reporting as ordered, Sir."

The Colonel nodded his head and extended his hand. "Colonel Miller, Lieutenant," he said, shaking hands. "Come into my office and we will discuss the coming events.

Andrew looked at the portly Colonel and once again wondered what the hell he was doing there, but he held his tongue, knowing that sooner or later he would find out what was going on. He followed the Colonel to his office, all the time feeling the eyes of the receptionist on his back. The Colonel opened the door and they stepped in. "Take a chair, Lieutenant," Miller said sitting at his desk. "May I offer you refreshments?" he asked, his eyebrow raised in question.

"No Sir, nothing for me," Andrew said, sitting on a hard chair in front of the desk. He wanted to know what was going on, get this over with and he waited patiently while Colonel Miller thumbed through a file.

"You are twenty-four years old," he said, a statement, not a question.

"Yes, Sir."

"And you enlisted in the Army from Stonewall, Texas," he said, again a statement and Andrew realized the man had his 201 file in front of him.

"With all due respect, Sir," Andrew said, "what is this all about?"

The Colonel put the file down and looked at him with a puzzled expression on his face.

"You really don't know, do you?" he asked.

"No, Sir, I don't have any idea why I've been ordered to Ft. Myer."

The Colonel chuckled, his eyes laughing and then he said, "Well son, tomorrow at 0900 hours the President of the United States will award you a medal." He paused for a second, his eyes fixed on the young man in front of him and then, he continued. "The Medal of Honor, Lieutenant."

Andrew heard those words and his mouth went dry. For a second he was unable to talk. His heart beat faster and his eyes became moist. He stood there, his mouth hanging open and then a smile flickered across his face. He thought about his father and Catherine and finally came back to earth.

Colonel Miller was looking at him with an amused expression on his face. "The cat got your tongue, Lieutenant?" he said, laughing. "Let me be the first to congratulate you."

"Thank you, Sir," he said, his mind numbed by the unexpected news. The Medal of Honor, he thought, the highest honor a soldier could receive from his nation, and he was going to get one. He was elated at first and then he thought that no one really cared, there was no one to share the news with and his heart felt dejected. He noticed the Colonel looking at him intently and he controlled his feelings.

"Anything wrong, Lieutenant?" Miller asked.

"No, Sir, just thinking," he said.

"I know you must be tired so we will go over some of the things briefly about the ceremony and then you are on your own," he said.

Andrew nodded his head in ascent and Colonel Miller busied himself with paperwork. He searched for something on his cluttered desk, finally finding it he started reading.

"These are your orders putting you on TDY (temporary duty) status with me for thirty days. Also a pay voucher and check that you have to sign for before you leave tonight and this is your authorization to go to the Post supply room and draw another set of Army issues. You are to present yourself tomorrow at this office in Class "A" uniform with all your authorized medals and decorations." He paused looking for another paper and then he continued reading. "By Army authorization you are entitled to wear the Combat Infantry Badge, the Purple Heart medal, the Korea Expeditionary medal, the Army Commendation medal and the National Defense, also all your badges of marksmanship earned during Basic Training and Advance Training." He stopped again looking for more papers and finally raised his head, looking at Andrew. "Any questions, Lieutenant?" he asked.

No, Sir, not right now," Andrew said.

"That's fine, then Lieutenant," Miller said coming to his feet. "You are to stay at the OBAQ (Officers Bachelors Quarters) for officers and I'll see you tomorrow at 0800 hours. I'll have my Sergeant drop you at the Post Exchange where you can buy whatever you need for tomorrow."

Andrew got up too, coming to attention. "If the Colonel doesn't mind, Sir," he said, "I would rather walk. I've been sitting in a bus for almost three days and I'm kind of stiff."

"That's fine Lieutenant," Miller said, "whatever you want."

Andrew turned around exiting the office and made his way out, noticing that the receptionist's desk was empty. Once outside he stopped for a second, breathing in deeply of the cold air. He consulted the small map of the Post that the Colonel had given him while lighting a cigarette, noticing that the PX was not too far away from where he stood. He started walking in that general direction when he felt someone next to him. He glanced behind him and saw the slender figure of the girl at the reception desk approaching him. She was taller than what he thought, he realized, looking at her long legs. She was dressed in a simple black ankle-length dress, high heel pumps on her feet. She stopped next to him and Andrew looked in her eyes. They reminded him of Catherine's eyes, full of laughter and mischief and he felt a pang of regret.

"Hi," she said, coming to stand by his side.

"Hi yourself," Andrew said, waiting. She seemed to vacillate for a second and then she looked at him and went on.

"You want some company?" she asked, the look in her eyes unmistakable. For a moment Andrew thought about rejecting the offer. It had been a long time since he had female company and the woman in front of him was young and pretty. What the hell, he thought, it would not do any harm. He nodded his head in ascent and the young woman smiled deeply, blushing.

Together they made their way, Andrew breathing the heady smell of her perfume, thinking that it was nice to hear a female voice next to him. To his surprise he found out that she owned a car, a couple of years old, but in good shape, parked behind the building.

"Well," he said, getting in, "the army must pay the civilian help better than they pay us."

"Not bad," she said smiling, "not bad at all."

This was looking like a very promising evening, he thought, casting glances at the woman. He found out that her name was Gloria Talbott and had been employed at the Post for a couple of years. She lived alone in a small apartment just off the Post and after Andrew had finished his Army business they went out to eat and to celebrate his award. She was good company, making him relax and for a while taking his mind off the ever present memory of Catherine Weatherly.

When the evening was over Andrew walked her to her apartment. They stood in the door and she raised her head to look at him better in the semi-darkness of the entrance. She was tall, but he still had several inches over her, her head reaching up to his mouth. The man intrigued her. He was polite and quiet, much too quiet for one so young and her curiosity was piqued. She knew he liked what he saw but so far he had been the perfect gentleman. Not that she was a hussy, throwing herself at the first man she saw, but this one was different, she could sense it.

She fixed her lavender eyes on him and in a voice husky with desire she asked, "You want to come in?"

Andrew saw her standing there, smelling of fresh flowers and enticing, and for a moment his manhood reacted to her. He reached for her, his mouth covering hers, his tongue searching, probing. She arched her body to him, grinding against him, feeling him grow hard and she moaned, a deep, arousing sound that sent his blood rushing through his veins like a raging fire. And then, the image of a beautiful woman, her face lifted to him, smiling, came into his mind and he pulled back, his chest rising and falling with each breath, his heart beating a wild crescendo in his chest. He ran his fingers through his short hair and looked at her, regret in his eyes.

"I'm sorry, Gloria," he said, seeing the bewilderment in her face. "I'm no good for this."

"But…but what's wrong?" she asked perplexed at the behavior now. "Have I done something wrong?"

"It's not you," he said with a deep sigh, "it's not you at all." He stood still for a minute, wanting to explain, but unable to, and then, he whirled around, his shoulders sagging.

Gloria Talbott saw him go and she shook her head in wonderment, finally shrugging her shoulders and going into her apartment. This was the first time in her life that she had been turned down and she wondered who was responsible for the pain she had seen in his eyes, what woman had plunged the knife in him to make him what he was now.

# 18

The White House
Washington, DC
12 January 1951
0900 Hours

    Lt. Colonel Miller and Lt. Beck made their way to the White House in almost complete silence, each one deep in his own thoughts. They had become entangled in traffic due to an accident on the highway and they were almost late arriving. Several other medal recipients were there also and Andrew was the last one to arrive. The ceremony was taking place outside of the White House in the Rose Garden, and the military and the press were in attendance, the occasion festive. According to Colonel Miller his award was to be the last one, his was the only Medal of Honor to be given and Andrew felt some apprehension at that. He didn't like crowds and he was hoping that the ceremony would be fast. The President was going to pin the Medal on him and he was anxious about that too. The President of the United States, imagine that, Andrew thought, wishing his father could be here.

They walked around for a few minutes, Colonel Miller introducing him to some of the brass and press reporters and then it was time. There were four other recipients in line, two for the Distinguished Service Cross and Purple Hearts and two for the Silver Star and several other lesser medals. Then it would be his turn. The day was crisp, not too cold and the sun cast a brilliant light over the ceremony making it feel almost warm.

The soul stirring notes of the National Anthem started and the assembly came to attention. A few seconds later the President of the United Sates came strolling down and then there was silence.

An Army officer, a Major resplendent in his class A's strode to a podium in the center of the garden and immediately started reading. One by one the soldiers to Andrew's right moved forward to receive their medals, the flash of light bulbs everywhere. And then, for a few seconds there was silence one more time. The Army band played some Army tunes and then it stopped, the President of the United States getting up from his chair and standing by the podium, the Army Major at his side.

The Major looked at the paper in front of him and in a loud commanding voice he started, "Second Lieutenant Andrew Beck," he roared, "front and center." Andrew heard his name and he swallowed hard, starting to walk toward the President.

He stopped three feet away from the major, coming to attention, all six feet three inches of him ramrod straight, his eyes several inches above the President's head and he saluted.

"Sir, Second Lt. Andrew Beck reporting," he said, noticing how short the President was. His salute was returned and he remained at attention, listening to the Major reading his citation.

Rank and Organization: Second Lt. Andrew Beck (then PFC), U.S. Army,

                      Able Company, 19th Infantry Regiment.
Date and Place: Near Hangnyong, South Korea, 11 November 1950.

Entered Service at: Stonewall, Texas
Born: 19 January 1927, Stonewall, Texas.
General Order No. 69, 12 January 1951.
Citation: Second Lt. Andrew Beck, Able Company distinguished himself by conspicuous intrepidity and gallantry, above and beyond the call of duty in action against hostile forces. At approximately 0300 hours, Lt. Beck's company, holding an outpost some 150 yards in front of enemy lines came under a ferocious mortar and artillery attack, followed by a charge of an estimated 350 enemy troops. Intense small arms, machine-gun, hand grenade and mortar fire all along the front line forced the company to seek the shelter of the trenches. During the fight, Lt. Beck, already wounded by grenade fragments, refused medical treatment in order to continue assisting the company. With his platoon sergeant dead and his company commander wounded, Lt. Beck observed the enemy breaching the trenches. Lt. Beck leaped to his feet, pouring rifle and BAR fire on the enemy, killing them by the score. Urging the remaining troops to charge the enemy, Lt. Beck charged the hostile force with indomitable courage. Within yards of the enemy, Lt. Beck was knocked to the ground when a bullet pierced his thigh. Ignoring the wound he jumped to his feet and continued to close with the enemy in hand-to-hand combat. Shouting to his fellow soldiers he charged the enemy time and time again, inflicting heavy casualties with rifle butt and bayonet on the enemy force, causing the fanatical foe to withdraw. Lt. Beck's superb leadership, incredible courage, and consummate devotion to the call of duty so inspired his fellow comrades that the enemy attack was completely halted, saving his company and battalion from possible disaster. His sustained personal bravery and indomitable fighting spirit against overwhelming odds reflect the utmost glory upon

himself and uphold the finest traditions of the infantry and the United States Army."

There was complete silence when the Major finished reading the citation, all eyes glued to the young man standing in front of the President.

Then the Major's voice was heard again, the President moving around in front of Andrew, a small case in his hand.

"By order of the President of the United States, the Medal of Honor is hereby awarded to Lt. Andrew Beck."

The President opened the small box and took the medal out. Andrew looked at the medal in the hands of the President and thought that he had never seen anything that had so much tradition and meaning in his life. He had heard a lot about the medal, but never seen one before and now he looked at the one in the President's hand with awe.

The Medal was a bronze star, surrounded by a green laurel wreath suspended from a bronze bar on which the word "valor" was inscribed, surmounted by an eagle. In the center of the star was the head of Minerva, Roman goddess of righteous war and wisdom, surrounded by the words "United States of America." There were green oak leaves on each ray of the star. The President unfolded the small sash holding the medal and taking a step forward, raised his arms to place it around Andrew's neck. Andrew bowed his head slightly in order to make it easier and then the President was shaking his hand, congratulating him.

"Well done son," he said, his voice deep and resonant, looking at Andrew.

"Thank you, Sir," he said, noticing the strong grip of the President's hand. He returned to attention and the band played another tune. When it was over Andrew looked around the ceremonial grounds. Colonel Miller was in deep conversation with some officer and Andrew waited, shaking hands with several people. He was about to walk toward Miller when he felt a strong hand on his shoulder and he whirled around, coming face to face with Colonel Devlin. A smile of pleasure broke across Andrew's face and then he came to attention, snapping a perfect salute. Colonel Devlin returned it and then immediately extended his hand.

"Congratulations Lieutenant," he said, his voice soft, affectionate. And then he came to attention, saluting the medal as was customary.

Andrew looked at him closely, noticing the man had aged since the last time he saw him, and had been promoted too. He noticed the eagle of a full bird Colonel on Devlin's shoulders and smiled. He liked this man and for some reason, he believed that the Colonel had some affection for him too.

"I believe congratulations are in order for you too, Sir," he said, his head nodding toward the eagle.

"Thank you, son," he said, taking Andrew's arm and walking toward a waiting sedan.

"It happened after the battle in which you performed so gallantly," he said, walking side by side. People were dispersing, getting into cars and presently there were only a handful of people left.

"I have to be on my way to Korea tonight, but I wanted to be present for your ceremony," he said, "and to give you some fatherly advice." He stopped walking and turned to face Andrew.

"You are an officer now," he started, "and I believe that you will go far, son. All you have to do is do your duty, keep your nose clean, and get an education." He paused for a second, watching Miller heading in their direction and he continued. "You have thirty days to do this Public Relations tour, so do your best, make your speeches and shake the hands and after that, you can name your duty station."

"I just want to get back to my unit, Sir," Andrew said, "and do my job."

"Well, you can if you want to. I'll be there for a few more months and then it's back to the States."

Lt. Colonel Miller approached, stopping in front of them and seeing the silver eagle on Devlin's shoulder came to attention, saluting his superior officer. Devlin returned his salute and then extended his hand.

"I'm Colonel Devlin," he said, giving Miller a blue eye stare, measuring the man.

"Lt. Colonel Miller, sir, at your service."

Miller looked at Andrew, his eyes asking the question, wondering what was the connection between the two of them.

"Colonel Devlin is my battalion commander, Sir," he said, seeing Miller's eyebrow raised in recognition.

"Colonel Devlin," he said, "yes, I remember now, sir. Your name was the principal one involved with our young Medal of Honor winner."

Devlin didn't answer, just nodded his head. He looked at his watch and started walking toward his car, taking Andrew's arm again. "You must excuse me, Colonel," he said to Miller. "I need a few seconds of this young man's time. Miller stopped where he was, saluting Devlin again. "You take your time Colonel," he said, walking a distance away from them.

"I have an appointment at the Pentagon," Devlin said. "So I must be going now. You remember what I told you and keep your nose clean." He stopped, extending his hand, his grip dry and strong.

"You know," he said, his voice soft. "I had a son, about your age. He was killed in Normandy." For a moment Andrew was lost, seeing the pain reflected in the man's eyes and then the memories were gone and Devlin shook his head. He looked at Andrew's face and stepped back, his hand coming up in a perfect salute to the man and the medal. Andrew returned it and Devlin did an about face and was gone.

# 19

19th Infantry Regiment
South Korea
20 February 1951

    Second Lieutenant Beck arrived in Korea after his thirty days TDY ready for whatever was coming. He had spent the last few days making speeches and shaking hands until everything was a blur. He had danced and told stories at so many functions in Washington that he and the other GIs felt like they were on a show. He understood the need for the Army to show them off, but was relieved when Colonel Miller had finally announced that the tour was over. As predicted by Colonel Devlin he was asked for his choice of assignments and he had requested Korea, making Miller shake his head at the choice.

    "You can go anywhere you want, Lieutenant," Miller had said, "why go back to that stinking, frozen piece of earth?"

    "Because it is my duty, Sir," Andrew said, knowing well that the paper pushers didn't have any idea what he was talking about. And now he was getting his wish. The same unit also, he thought, maybe they could give him news of Paul.

After three days of traveling he finally made it to the battalion CP. It was really cold and once again it was raining when he arrived, his breath steaming and he sought the shelter of the bunker. He noticed that conditions had improved some in the front lines with more tents for the troops and that every GI that he saw was equipped for cold weather. He paused for a second at the entrance of the CP and then walked in, his eyes adjusting slowly to the interior. He saw several people in the place, all busy with one task or another and two men hunched over a field table. He walked to the table and stood still until finally one of the men noticed him and looked at him.

"What can I do for you, Lieutenant?" he said, Andrew noticing that it was a Lt. Colonel. He came to attention and saluted, "Lt. Andrew Beck, reporting for duty, Sir,"

The Colonel raised his hand in a barely noticeable salute, looking at Andrew's chest. He was wearing the CIB on his field jacket and nothing else, his nametag on the right.

At the mention of his name the other soldier raised his head, a smile on his face and Andrew heard the voice of Colonel Devlin.

"I can't believe my eyes," he said, coming around the table, "if it isn't our hero." Andrew smiled at seeing the old warrior, coming to attention once more, and saluting. "This is Lt. Beck, Pierce," he said, addressing the Colonel next to him, "our Medal of Honor winner."

"Nice meeting you, Lieutenant," he said, extending his hand. "Heard a lot about you."

"Thank you, Sir," Andrew said.

"I'm glad you are here, son," Devlin said. "I sure can use you." They exchanged pleasantries for a few more minutes and then Devlin put his hand on Andrew's arm and said, "Let's take a walk outside Lieutenant. Give Colonel Pierce your orders and then I'll have my driver take you back to your old company. You are now a platoon leader in Able Company."

Andrew did as he was told and then they walked outside. It was almost dark and it was still raining, slow drizzle that looked like it would never end.

"I'm not going to paint you a pretty picture, Andrew," Devlin said, using his name in a familiar way. "MacArthur is trying hard to get us moving, but everything is so fucked up now that I doubt if we make any progress before spring gets here. We are short of almost everything, but the situation is slowly getting better. Still you will not have a full compendium of troops and the enemy is still out there." He paused, fishing for a cigarette and offering one to Andrew. They lit up and Devlin continued walking, finally stopping at the field kitchen, smoke rising from a pipe in the center. "Let's get some coffee," he said, walking inside. It was fairly warm and they approached a heavyset mess Sergeant.

"Got any of that piss water, Charlie," Devlin said, a smile flickering across his stern features.

"Yes Sir, just made some. Sit down and I'll get you both a cup."

They sat down on a bench and Andrew realized how tired he was. He had barely slept any in the last three days and it was beginning to get to him. The coffee came with cream and sugar and they sipped the hot liquid. Devlin blew on his cup and then fixing his blue eyes on Andrew continued talking.

"Captain Albert is your company commander. Good guy but still green, so watch it and help him all you can." They talked for a while, Andrew forcing himself to listen to Devlin, his mind craving sleep.

The heat and the talking finally got to him and his head rolled, jerking himself awake. "Damn, I'm sorry, Colonel," he said, embarrassed at his manners.

"I'm the one who is sorry, son," Devlin said, getting up. "I didn't take into consideration that you must be tired." He put his gloves and hat on saying, "Stay here, finish your coffee, I'll get my driver and have him come and get you and take you up front. I'll come by tomorrow or the next day and see how you are doing."

Andrew got up, saluting the Colonel and then he was back on the bench finishing his coffee. How long he waited he didn't know, but he was sound asleep when the driver finally came, a blanket over him. The mess Sergeant must have put it on him, Andrew thought, looking around to thank him. The man was gone and he and the Staff Sergeant made their way out, climbing in the jeep and making their way to Able Company position.

They arrived in a few minutes and Andrew found the CP. Entering, he reported to the company clerk. Staff Sergeant Ramirez was typing on a sheet of paper when he saw the Second Lieutenant walk in. Another cherry, he thought, and then his eyes caught the CIB on the man's chest and he looked at him with renewed interest.

"May I help you?" he said and then, after a pair of steel gray eyes fixed on him he added, "Sir."

"Yes you may, Sergeant," the Lieutenant said, his eyes taking in the interior of the bunker. Human forms were lying around with blankets and ponchos covering most of them, a stove in the center radiating some heat. "I'm reporting in." And then, without waiting for a reply he asked, "Where is Captain Albert?"

"He is over there, Sir," Staff Sergeant Ramirez said, pointing at several men huddled together on a corner. "He is the one sleeping on the cot." Once again he omitted saying Sir and the cold eyes fixed on him again. He saw the look and he swallowed hard, the word "Sir," coming out of his mouth.

"Let's remember our military courtesy, Sergeant," the Lieutenant said softly, walking toward the sleeping figure on the cot.

Damn, Sergeant Ramirez thought, who the fuck is that mean looking son of a bitch? He looked at the man walking toward the end of the bunker and he shivered, thinking about those cold gray eyes. He might be a lowly Second Lieutenant, Ramirez thought, but cheery he is not.

He saw the man reach the cot, bend down and shake the Captain. As the Captain woke up and rubbed his eyes, the Lieutenant came to attention, snapping a salute and then he was at ease, waiting.

Andrew saw the man waking up and he looked at him, sizing him up. Captain Albert was short and barrel-chested, with a thin pencil line mustache on his lip. He was young, probably thirty something, Andrew thought, noticing the dark lines under the eyes. And under a lot of stress, he thought again.

"Lt. Beck reporting for duty, Sir," he said, saluting his superior officer. Captain Roberts looked up and finally stood, reaching for the copy of the orders that Andrew handed him. He put gold-rimmed glasses on his face and looked at Andrew one more time before he read the orders.

"Glad you are here, Beck," he said and then he looked toward Ramirez. "Get the Lieutenant a place to sleep for tonight." To Andrew he said, "We will talk tomorrow." Saying that he fell down on the cot and was snoring within seconds. Andrew looked at him and shook his head wondering about the man.

Ramierz approached him. "If the Lieutenant will come with me, I'll show you a place to sleep, Sir." Andrew nodded his head in ascent and turned around, indicating he was ready to go.

"Lead the way, Sergeant, lead the way." They were on their way out when they almost collided with a man walking in. In the semi-darkness of the bunker Andrew thought that the man was familiar and he took a step back in order to see the man better. "Oh shit, I'm sorry," the man said, removing his helmet, running his hand over his short hair.

The moment Andrew heard the man's voice his face broke into a grin and he reached over, grabbing him in a bear hug.

The man pulled back in surprised, listening to the Lt. laugh. Ramirez wondered if the Lieutenant was going crazy.

"Paul Ragsdale, you sorry excuse for a GI," the Lieutenant said, and then Paul Ragsdale was laughing too and the two men were slapping each other on the back, talking at the same time. They heard murmurs from the men sleeping and the two of them finally stopped trying to kill each other.

"Ramierz, this is Andrew Beck, our Medal of Honor hero," he said, "and my friend."

"I had the pleasure of meeting the Lieutenant," he said and something in his tone made Paul aware that everything hadn't been smooth.

"You already making waves?" Paul asked, his eyes laughing. He didn't wait for a response, his hand reached for Andrew's arm and pulled on him. "I'll take care of the Lieutenant," he said.

They walked out and spent the next couple of hours catching up with each other. Paul was glad that Andrew had come back to his same old company and Andrew found out that his friend was now a platoon Sergeant, having been promoted after receiving the Purple Heart and a Bronze Star for valor. They talked for a while until Paul asked about Catherine, and he saw the look on Andrew's face. His voice became serious and soft. He told Paul everything that had happened or at least what he thought happened and after that they never brought up the subject of Catherine Weatherly again.

Pusan, South Korea
15 August 1951

For the next six months after his arrival he was the Platoon Leader for 1st Platoon and after Captain Roberts was killed in action, he became acting Company Commander. There were more battles and more daring missions, another Purple Heart and a Bronze Star for valor, until finally one day the top brass thought it was about time to get Lt. Beck out of the line of fire. After all he was a Medal of Honor winner and it would not look good to the folks back home or the press if he were killed in action in Korea. Devlin had requested a promotion for him to 1st Lieutenant, and when that came through he was transferred to the States. The day of his departure found he and Paul sitting in the company jeep, waiting for his transport plane to depart.

The two friends shared a cigarette and waited in the sultry heat for other GIs to board the plane.

"This damn place kills me," Paul said, sitting on the driver's side, smoke drifting from the cigarette dangling from his lips. "If the cold don't get you the heat will." Andrew didn't answer, his eyes following the planes coming in and out of the small airstrip. Over and over planes landed, disgorging men and material, workers moving like ants, unloading the equipment, the noise almost overpowering.

When it was time for him to go he dropped the cigarette to the tarmac, his boot crushing the butt and grinding it down.

He stood still for a second, sweat running down his face, the scar on the right side of his head visible now that his hair was cut extremely short. His skin was tanned to a deep golden shade and there were fine lines in the corners of his eyes. He turned to Paul and extended his hand, a look of sadness etched on his handsome face.

"I'll let you know where I am and you try to get there," he said, shaking Paul's hand. They had talked about trying to serve together in the same places and this was the first time that would be put to the test.

Andrew heard the propellers start on his plane and he bent over hefting his duffel bag to his shoulder. Paul looked at him, a crooked smile on his face and then, he came to attention, snapping a salute to his friend. Andrew returned it, smiling too.

"Take care," he said.

For a second he held Paul's gaze and then he whirled around, boarding the plane. Paul J. Ragsdale saw him go and he wondered when he would lay eyes on his friend again.

# 20

Fort Benning, Georgia
17 September 1961
1400 hours

Andrew Beck stood at the door of the C-117 plane, the raw wind making him shiver. His eyes were mere slits and he looked out and down seeing the wheat fields rolling by him as the plane leveled at 1,500 feet. Everything was noise and confusion as the long stick of paratroopers stood in line for the fifth and final jump, the jumpmaster checking static lines and equipment. This was their last jump before graduating from jump school at Fort Benning and Andrew was looking forward to finishing. He was due at Fort Lee Virginia for Rigger School in a few days and before that he wanted to spend some time with Paul Ragsdale and his wife.

The years had been kind to him. At thirty-four he looked the same as he always had, the boyish good looks still holding. After Korea he had come home to different assignments and through the years he had managed to get a college education, going to school in his spare time and attending every school the Army had to offer. The railroad tracks of a Captain could be seen on his collar and the Ranger tab on his shoulder. He had been there for Paul when he finally got married to his sweetheart, Lynn, after coming back from Korea. The ceremony had taken place in Fort Rucker, Alabama, where Paul had been assigned and Andrew had managed to show up in time to be the best man. After that, Paul had been assigned to Fort Benning Infantry School while Andrew had gone to become the XO (Executive Officer) for an aviation company at Rucker.

He felt the hand of the jumpmaster on his shoulder and turned to look at him. There was no way to talk in the plane, the noise from the propellers absolutely infernal. He saw the grizzled old Sergeant raise his hand indicating two minutes from the drop zone and once again he looked out ready to go. He felt the hand on his shoulder again and looked up to see the green light on the door and felt a whack across his buttocks. He jumped, feeling the incredible rush of adrenaline coursing through his body, the T-10 opening, jerking him up and then he was floating, looking at other paratroopers exiting the aircraft. He was descending at 22 feet per second and he didn't have long to wait before the ground came up to meet him. He did a PLF (parachute landing fall) landing hard, the impact taking the breath out of him and he lay on the hard ground exhilarated, knowing that from that day on the silver wings of a paratrooper would be part of him. When he regained his breath he stood up, rolling his parachute and walking to the assembly point. Once there he turned in his parachute, waiting for the others to come on. He walked a distance from the others and lit a cigarette. I've been trying all my life to quit these things, he thought taking a drag, and I still can't do it.

He was immersed in his thoughts that he had made the right choice by staying in the Army. He had done well and besides that, he thought, the Army is the only family I know, the only friends I have.

He finished the cigarette noticing that the other troopers were about to form and he crushed the butt, making sure it was completely out before putting it in his pocket.

He joined the others, everyone happy to be finished, ready for something else. He saw Lieutenant Colonel White, the school commandant, approaching, the instructors calling to attention and the company forming, ready to receive the silver wings. The ceremony was over in no time. A short speech, the wings pinned on the chest, a hand shake and a well wish and in minutes it was over, troopers heading in every direction, family coming over to hug and kiss the new paratroopers, wives congratulating husbands. He stood still watching the activity around him, feeling the loneliness that times like this brought to him, until a voice at the back made him turn around, his face braking into a grin.

"You are going to have to get married so I can quit coming to all these damn schools you have attended," Paul Ragsdale said, coming to attention and saluting his friend.

Andrew saluted back, looking intently at his friend. The tall, skinny kid of Korea was now the tall, extremely well built man, twenty-nine years old. He was clean-shaven and his hair was short, his blue eyes full of life and laughter as usual. His fatigues were starched to a cardboard finish and the jump boots gleamed. On his chest right above U.S. Army was the silver wings of a paratrooper and above that the CIB badge…

It's good to see you too, Paul," Andrew said, looking around.

"If you are looking for that glorious wife of mine," he said, "forget it. She is at home making you a cake and cooking up a storm. She said for me to be sure you are brought home immediately."

Andrew laughed shaking his head and they started walking toward the parking lot. Most everyone else was gone, with just a detail of GIs loading a truck with parachutes. They had not seen each other for several years now and were eager to get reacquainted. They talked often on the phone and Andrew had spent some leave time with them, but time was always in short supply. They had planned this little reunion after

Andrew notified Paul that he would be coming to Benning for jump school. They found Paul's car, got in and in a few minutes were rolling toward the post housing area. Thirty minutes later they were home. Lynn had drinks ready and pronounced that the food would be ready in an hour. Andrew took the opportunity to clean up, changing into clean fatigues and then dinner was ready. They shared the food and the talk, remembering good times and bad times, reinforcing the friendship that had taken them along so many different routes and after two days Andrew Beck was gone again, answering the call of duty, wherever it took him. Paul and Lynn saw him go as they had done many times before in the years after the war, wondering if the man would ever settle down, find a woman and fall in love. They both knew that there had been women in his life, probably too many, but as far as anything serious that had not happened. Andrew Beck was still in love with the only woman he could never have.

Ft. Bragg, North Carolina
15 April 1962

After Ft. Lee, Virginia there had been a transfer to Ft. Bragg, North Carolina, where he was assigned to a Quartermaster Company, attached to the 82nd Airborne Division and for a while he was content, going about the daily duties of running a company and bored to death.

But all that was about to change soon. He had come in early one Monday morning going through the mountain of paperwork and grumbling about it when his phone rang. He let it ring several times before he threw the pen down and grabbed the damn thing, stopping the noise.

"Captain Beck speaking," he said, reaching for his coffee mug.

"Captain, this is Lt. Wolf, aide-de-camp to Major General Devlin, Assistant Chief of Staff."

"What can I do for you, Lieutenant?" he asked, wondering what an aide-de-camp wanted from him and suddenly he put a face to the name. Devlin, his old battalion commander. Well, he thought chuckling; the old man had done well.

"General Devlin would like the pleasure of your company for lunch at the officers club, Sir," the Lieutenant said, "around 1230 hours, Sir."

Andrew was pleasantly surprised that Devlin still remembered him and wondered what this was all about. This was a command, not just a request.

"Tell the General that I'll be there, Lieutenant," he said, "and that it will be my pleasure." He hung up the phone, his mind mulling over the unexpected call. What would Devlin want from him? Andrew thought, getting up and pouring himself another cup of coffee. He sipped it carefully, looking at his watch. Well, whatever it was he would find out soon he thought, going back to his paperwork.

At precisely 1230 hours he came into the officer's club, his eyes searching for the familiar figure. He was still looking among the crowd when a 1st Lieutenant approached him, a smile on his young face. "Captain Beck?" he asked, his eyebrows raised in question.

Andrew nodded his head in the affirmative.

"Follow me please, Sir. The General is waiting," he said, whirling around and heading for the mess. Andrew followed and shortly thereafter he came face to face with Major General Devlin sitting at a table in a private dining room. He saw the eyes fixed on him, a look of approval and pride registering in his eyes and Andrew felt a surge of affection for the old warrior. Devlin came to his feet upon seeing him, extending his hand. Andrew shook it, feeling the still strong grip and his face lightened up with a smile of pleasure.

"How are you, son?" Devlin asked, his eyes taking in the young man in front of him.

"I'm fine, General, thank you, Sir," he said, noticing the two stars on Devlin's shoulders. "I believe congratulations are in order?" he stated, indicating the stars. "And how are you, Sir?"

"Thank you, son. I'm doing just fine, Andrew, just fine," Devlin said, a mischievous smile on his face now. "Sit down and let's eat something."

Andrew sat down noticing that the aide-de-camp had mysteriously disappeared and again his mind started wondering.

They talked about old days for a while and their respective careers until the food came. The General was obviously in a good mood, talking about his family and his new job at the Pentagon and finally, once the meal was over, he pulled a couple of cigars from a box and offered one to Andrew. A waitress came in, refilling their coffee cups, setting ashtrays in front of them and finally leaving, closing the door softly after her. They lit the cigars and General Devlin sat back, relaxed. And then he started.

"Have you ever heard of Vietnam?" he asked, puffing on his cigar.

"Yes, Sir, I have," he answered, wondering where Devlin was going with this. "A French colony, until they were defeated by the Vietnamese, later partitioned into South and North."

"Right," Devlin said. "North Vietnam is communist and the South, more or less democratic. And now we have advisors helping the South fight a war against the North." He paused for a while, his forehead creased in thought. "The President requested the Chief of Staff to send someone over there to get a first hand look at what is really going down. He wants a military man and a military point of view. I was assigned to get that man and I thought of you."

"Me? Why me, Sir?" he asked, confused. "Obviously there are other men out there more qualified than I am for this type of mission."

"I've been impressed by your devotion to duty and your code of ethics, son, and I believe that you are the right man for this mission. I believe that you have what it takes. We want the truth about what the situation really is over there, no washouts and no sugar coating." He paused again, sipping his coffee slowly, his eyes fixed on Andrew. "Besides, I kind of liked the idea of you and me working together again, like old times." He stopped talking giving Andrew a chance to digest the words and then he continued, "So I set out to find you and when I did I read your 201 file and like I said, I'm still impressed. You have come far Andrew and I would like to have you working with me." He blew some more smoke and waited for a reaction from Andrew. When none came, he continued, "Now the question is, do you want it?"

Andrew was silent for a minute, his mind pondering the implications. He had heard bits and pieces about the country and the situation over there and thought that he would like to go. Besides, he was bored to pieces now, and a change would be good for him.

"Yes, Sir. I think I would," he said, a smile on his face now.

"Good, that settles that," General Devlin said, getting up. At that moment the door opened and Lt. Wolf came in and approached the table.

"We need to go, Sir," he said, looking at his watch.

"Right, Pete," Devlin said and then leaned over to the side picking up a brief case from a chair, extracting a heavy folder from it. "This is classified information and 'Top Secret'." Familiarize yourself with it, it will give you a feeling for what you are about to do." He paused, his eyebrow raised in thought. "I have another meeting to attend with the base commander and then it's back to Washington. Lt. Wolf will stay with you, brief you and get that folder back today." He extended his hand, a smile etched on his face.

It's good to have you on board, Andrew," he said.

"Thank you, Sir. I'll try not to disappoint you." He came to attention and even if he wasn't expected to salute inside a building, he did. Devlin returned the salute and without preamble, he exited the room.

"If the Captain would bear with me, I'll be happy to brief you, Sir," Wolf said. Andrew gave a consenting nod with his head and sat down again, wondering now what he had gotten into this time.

"These are your orders placing you on TDY (temporary duty assignment) for thirty days, starting tomorrow," Wolf said, handing Andrew a set of orders. You will be traveling VOCG (verbal order, commanding general) by General Devlin until you arrive at the Pentagon.

There orders will be cut for your travel to South Vietnam. You will travel in civilian clothes and you will accompany a delegation of State Department officials," he paused, handing Andrew another file.

"Familiarize yourself with the contents," Wolf said. "It will tell you about the mission and what your parameters would be. At the end of thirty days you will return to the Pentagon and report to the General. You are also expected to write a report in triplicate for the General's Staff and the President. Any questions?"

"None so far," Andrew said, looking at the heavy file in his hand. I'm supposed to read this today, he thought, wondering how much time he really had.

"I'm to stay with you while you read the file, Sir," Wolf said.

Andrew nodded his head again, lit a cigarette and opened the first page, starting to read. This is going to be fun, he thought, noticing the time.

Three hours later his brain mushed, he was finished. His major in college had been Political Science and now he was glad, shaking his head at the contents of the file. Politics, he thought, is really a dirty word. He returned the file to Lt. Wolf, getting up from the chair and stretching his limbs.

Lt. Wolf got up, closed the file and put it in his briefcase. It was then that Andrew noticed the chain attached to Wolf's wrist and the briefcase and he looked at Wolf with renewed interest.

"You are the General's aide?" he asked, knowing what the answer would be. There was the hint of a smile on Lt. Wolf's face and then he fixed his eyes on Andrew.

"Yes, Sir, that's what I am." He threw Andrew a mock salute and walked away. Yeah, in a pig's eye you are, Andrew thought, getting ready to leave. More like CIA, he thought, exiting the building. Once outside he stopped for a second, looking at his orders. And then it dawned on him, the orders had been ready and in the hands of Lt. Wolf before he had agreed to go, meaning that Devlin was sure that he would agree. He shook his head, smiling. Old Devlin knew him pretty well, Andrew thought, and had probably guessed correctly that Andrew was bored to death on his present assignment and would not hesitate to put himself in harms way if the opportunity presented itself. He put the orders in his pocket, wondering what this would bring to his life and walked away, ready for whatever was waiting for him.

# 21

South Vietnam
Ban Don, Central Highlands
30 April 1962

Andrew Beck woke up to the sound of rain hitting the tin roof of the building where he and the group of Special Forces men had taken shelter during the night. It was still dark and he could see the glow of a cigarette tip by the door, the shadow of a man barely perceptible in the gloom. One of Walter's men, Andrew thought, on guard. Looking at his watch he noticed the time, 0330 hours. By now he figured his ass was in a sling, having disobeyed the orders of the military attaché at the embassy in Saigon almost two weeks ago.

He had been in Vietnam for almost four weeks and for the first two weeks he hadn't been able to accomplish anything of what General Devlin had requested. Besides some riding around from Saigon, short trips that didn't provide him with any useful information, he had been unable to convince the military attaché that he needed free reign in order to observe what was going on. And it sure as hell was not going on at the capital, Andrew thought, hating the sounds and smells of Saigon.

He had kept his mouth shut and his eyes and ears open to anything that was useful, but as far as the South Vietnamese army was concerned, there was nothing going on, just some disgruntled farmers trying to incite chaos and revolution and some probes from North Vietnam around the provinces. They didn't have much of an army, Andrew thought, or much of a government and at times he didn't even know who was in charge.

He had spent two frustrating weeks in Saigon hampered by the restrictions put on him by the Embassy, when he finally decided that if he was going to get his mission accomplished he was going to have to take matters into his own hands. And so he did.

He had been nursing a drink at a local bar, blocks away from the Embassy when the chair next to him was pulled out and a medium height man with short-cropped hair sat next to him. The man was in civilian clothes and his face was dark from exposure to the sun and wind. His hands were large and strong, full of calluses. He sat down and looked around, his pale blue eyes missing nothing. He lit a cigarette and ordered a drink. Once again he looked around and his eyes rested lightly on Andrew, passing by and coming back again. The man was young, probably thirty years old or less, Andrew thought, and he exuded confidence, an intangible thing that was almost arrogance. It was early on Friday night and the place was not yet crowded. Most of the clientele were Vietnamese, with an occasional European face. A group of Americans could be overheard at one corner, their hard hats identifying them as oil or construction workers.

Andrew went back to his drinking until he heard a voice next to him.

"American?" the voice asked. Andrew turned around to face the young man.

"Yes, you?" he asked, this time measuring the man with his eyes. The pale blue eyes were clear, intelligent and the man was obviously also measuring Andrew.

"Yep, all the way from South Dakota," he said, raising his glass to Andrew. The man looked at his watch and then at the entrance, his eyes shifting nervously to the bar and again to the door. He took a drag from his cigarette, crushing it and lighting another one immediately. The man is nervous, Andrew thought.

"Waiting for someone?" he asked, his tone neutral.

The young man looked at him, a frown on his face. Instead of an answer, he got another question.

"Who are you with?"

"I'm sorry, I don't get the meaning," Andrew said.

"What are you doing in sunny Vietnam?" he asked, impatient now.

Andrew thought about that for a second and decided to come clean. "I'm Captain Beck, U.S. Army, on a special mission for the Pentagon."

The man's eyebrows went up in what was a characteristic gesture for him. "Well, that's nice to know. "I'm Captain Richard Walter, Special Forces, U.S. Army." Andrew looked at him, surprise registered on his face. He had heard of them, back at Bragg but had never met one. Walter extended his hand, shaking Andrew's and his face lit up with a smile. "So tell me, what are you doing here?"

"Mostly wasting my time," Andrew said. For the next thirty minutes they talked about Andrew's mission and the difficulties that he was experiencing, while Walter kept looking at the door every few minutes. In those thirty minutes Andrew got more information from the young captain about the ongoing situation in Vietnam than in all the rest of the time he had been in Saigon. They ordered fresh drinks and this time when Walter looked up there was a tall, skinny man, standing next to them. When Walter saw him his relief was apparent. He came out of his chair in one fluid movement, grasping the other man by the arm, and Andrew noticed how fast and quiet the man could move.

"How is he?" he asked. The other man didn't answer, his eyes shifting to Andrew.

Captain Walter followed his eyes and shrugged his shoulders. "This is Captain Beck. He is all right. This is Sergeant Foster." He fixed his eyes on the tall man and raised his eyebrow in a silent question.

Foster looked at Andrew and he saw the same arrogance and confidence on his face that he had noticed on Walter's. The man barely inclined his head to Andrew, his eyes showing something like contempt and then he turned to Walter again. "He is in bad shape. The doctor said he might lose his leg. Too much time, too much poison".

"Damn those sons of bitches," Walter said, slamming his fist on the counter, loud enough to turn faces toward them. He controlled himself with an effort. The Vietnamese bartender came by saying something in Vietnamese and Walter fired back in the same language. What ever was said the man inclined his head and turned around, leaving them alone. Andrew looked at the two men wondering what was going on.

Foster pulled up a chair and Walter pushed his drink toward him. The man took a swallow and put it down. For a minute everything was quiet, Andrew watching the emotions playing on Walter's face, the faraway look in his blue eyes.

Walter shook his head and his eyes fixed on Andrew.

"We have been operating in this area for about six months, a place called Ban Don," he started, "and ever since we have been getting hit and sniped at. We figured out that it was a group of Viet Cong, the local guerrilla fighters and on several occasions we tried to find them and come to grips with them, but somehow they always know where we are and when we go on patrol. About a month ago they ambushed one of our patrols and killed one of my men and several of our CIDG's (civil irregular defense group). We caught up with them and gave them a bloody nose, but the sniping and the ambushes didn't stop. And then three nights ago we were on patrol again. This time one of my Tech Sergeants stepped on a booby trap, a punji stick, and it took us two days to get him here. They have the nasty habit of putting human excrement on them and the leg got infected." He paused for a second, signaling the bartender over. He spoke in Vietnamese again and shortly afterwards, fresh drinks came.

"The young man was Bobby Wright," Walter continued. "A bright kid from New York. Wanted to be a doctor some day and now he is about to lose his leg." He took a drink, his eyes full of rage.

They were silent for a while, each one lost in their thoughts until Walter shook his head and announced, "I know this French hangout where the food is really good, anybody hungry?"

Both Foster and Andrew nodded their heads yes and all three of them got up to go. "I'll meet you guys outside," Andrew said, heading for the toilet. Foster and Walter walked outside, smelling the flavor of Saigon, looking at the multitude going by.

Walter lit a cigarette, taking a deep drag and exhaling.

"You still have friends in high places?" he asked Foster.

"Yes, I do," Foster replied, wondering where his Captain was going.

"Go check on our new friend, Beck, and find out if he is who he says he is. If he is, I think I'll invite him for a tour of the country with us."

"That's against regulations, Captain," Foster said, a smile on his face.

"Yeah, I know all about regulations," he said, watching Andrew coming toward them.

They all piled in the jeep and several minutes later they were at the place. Foster excused himself and was gone for about thirty minutes while Walter and Andrew had some more drinks. I have to slow this down, Andrew thought, his head beginning to feel the effects of too much booze. When Foster returned they ordered the food and to Andrew's surprise he found out that he really enjoyed it. This was his first time with French food and the taste was great. They made small talk, Andrew enjoying the company of soldiers again, after the stuffy heads from the State Department. Halfway through the meal, Foster disappeared again, and on his return he had a smug look on his face. The conversation turned to war and soon it was Korea, Foster asking all kinds of questions about it. He was twenty-seven years old and wanted to hear everything he could from one who had been there. He had enlisted at eighteen, but had missed the action.

When Andrew excused himself to go to the toilet, Foster smiled at Walter and inched his chair forward.

"Guess what?" he asked, the look on his face one of intense pleasure.

"What?" Walter said, looking at Foster, wondering what was making him so smug.

"Our boy is who he says he is and he's got the "medal"."

"He got the medal?" Walter asked, his eyebrows going up. "You mean the medal?"

"Yes Sir, the medal and a bunch of other ones to go with it," he said, chuckling. The Bronze Star, a bunch of Purple Hearts, Legions of Merit and on and on."

"Well I'll be damned," Walter said, surprise in his voice.

When Andrew returned he could tell that something had transpired concerning him. The attitude of both men had changed, like they had measured him and found him worthy. The look in Foster's eyes was one of respect, no longer disdainful and when he answered a question he said 'sir'.

They spent the rest of the night talking and drinking until Andrew's head started spinning and all of them realized that they had had enough for one night. They all piled up in the Jeep and with Foster driving they made it back to Andrew's hotel.

They shook hands all around, Andrew thinking that he had never met better soldiers anywhere when Walter looked at him with a funny look on his face and then out of the blue he asked, "Would you like to go with us for a couple of weeks? Accommodations are not five star and it could be dangerous to your health, but…"

Andrew was stunned by the request and then he smiled.

"Of course I would," he said, not believing his good luck. A trip like that would help him to fulfill his mission and to get the data that he needed.

"Be here at six. Foster will pick you up," Walter said, shaking hands and getting back in the Jeep. They roared out into the traffic while Andrew stood on the sidewalk. He shook his head at his good fortune and walked inside thinking that the military attaché would be royally pissed by tomorrow.

At precisely six o'clock he was outside, his head splitting. Too much alcohol and too little sleep, Andrew thought, shaking his head. He was dressed in civilian clothes, but had several changes of military uniforms in his bag, his toilet kit and a 1911 Colt .45 with four spare clips. Traffic was light at this time of the morning and he didn't have long to wait, the jeep screeching to a halt in front of him. Foster was at the wheel and he slowed down just enough for Andrew to jump in.

"Morning, Sir," he said and he was off, roaring back on the road, shifting gears like one possessed. They rode for half an hour, almost in complete silence and finally, Foster stopped at a small airfield. A helicopter was waiting, the rotors turning. Foster signaled Andrew to go and get in and shortly after, he followed. Walter was already in the chopper and as soon as Foster jumped in they took off. The flight lasted twenty minutes and Andrew spent his time looking out, the immense expanse of jungle beneath giving him plenty to think about. If the U.S. became involved in a conflict in this place, Andrew thought, logistics and re-supply would be a nightmare. The terrain was impressive to say the least with jungles and mountains, rivers and valleys and hardly any roads. Here and there he could see villages, farmers working in the fields.

The chopper finally landed at a small clearing and they got out, stretching. Foster unloaded several small packages and put them in Army rucksacks, three of them. Captain Walter approached Andrew and handed him a .30 caliber carbine. Andrew accepted it and looked at Walter, noticing that he also had one in his hand and Foster had some kind of machine gun with him. Then Walter pulled something from his pocket and put it on his head. Andrew looked at it, realizing it was a green beret, a small crest on it. Hefting their packs the three of them, with Walter leading the way, started walking a small trail and after fifteen minutes they reached a small village. Some of the tribesmen saw them coming and in a short amount of time they were surrounded. The villagers slapping them on the back, smiling and talking, happy to see them return.

"These are Montagnards and the village is called Ban Don," Walter said, gesturing at the small village. "There are about two hundred of them in this area, most of them in this outpost and nine of my men."

Walter led them to a small hut and left him on his own while he checked with his men. That night he got to meet them all and was impressed at the young men and their outlook at the situation they were in. They exuded confidence just like Walter and Foster did and all of them seemed to have a good grasp of the mission. As far as Andrew was concerned these soldiers were the best he had ever seen. Their discipline and motivation was incredible and he felt that he was among the best.

He spent the next several days going out with patrols and getting to know the area and the people. The tribesmen were friendly and looked at the Special Forces group as their own, sharing their food and living accommodations with them. On his second day with Walter they were sniped at, a Montagnard getting wounded and Walter had sent his men after the sniper. They came back half an hour later empty handed and discouraged. During the patrols they continued to find booby traps and several villagers came to them, their feet transfixed by punji sticks. Walter saw all these and he was full of rage, cursing up a storm. He started sending night patrols but to no avail, the Viet Cong disappeared into the jungle like they never existed. And today had not been any different, Andrew thought, thinking about the small child that had been killed. He got up from his pallet, careful not to wake any of the men. It was raining hard now, the sound on the tin roof louder. He fished for a cigarette and approached the guard, seeing that it was Sgt. Lopez.

Getting a light from him, Andrew walked outside, stopping right at the door, his nostrils flaring, smelling the myriad of odors coming from the jungle. In two more days he would be leaving, returning to Saigon and then back to the States. He probably was in deep trouble by now and might even get a court martial for this, he thought, throwing the butt down on the wet dirt and crushing it. He heard the noise of a child crying and his mind went back to the child who had been killed today. The damn sniper was somewhere close, Andrew thought, probably with the rest of the Viet Cong who had been plaguing this place.

He breathed the morning air, smelling the rain and the wood smoke and then his stomach fluttered and he looked around. There was not one fire anywhere in sight and the wind was coming from the jungle, a hundred yards in front of him. Without really thinking he went back inside, snatching his carbine and a flashlight with a red cover and then going back out. He looked at the sky, realizing that the rain would not stop for a while. He started walking, his nose probing the air. Within seconds the jungle had swallowed him and Andrew made his way carefully, the rain masking his movement, containing the noise of his passage. Slowly, carefully, he made his way, following the tenuous smell of smoke hanging in the air. His whole body was tense, ready for anything, his mind thinking about all the hunting trips back home, except that this hunting was for men. Just like animals, men will hunker down when it rains and he was hoping that the smell of smoke was from a campfire. None of Walter's men were outside the perimeter tonight, so there was a good chance that he was right. He continued searching, knowing he had come almost a mile until the smell of smoke was so strong that he knew he must be close. And then he found them.

Ahead of him there was a small clearing in the jungle and he was about to step in it when he heard a muffled cough. He froze in place, his heart beating wildly, adrenaline rushing through him like fire. He saw the dying fire, the smoke curling lazily upward. Slowly he let his eyes roam and then, a form rose from the ground and he heard coughing again and the form bending over, throwing something on the fire, flames leaping. In the seconds before the fire settled down again, he saw several forms lying under some makeshift shelters and then he lost his night vision and he closed his eyes. Stupid, he thought, knowing that he should have closed his eyes. He remained still for an eternity, his heart going wild, fear a living thing clutching at his entrails. He waited until he heard the man lie down again and then he opened his eyes, searching for guards. There weren't any, he realized. The Viet Cong were so confidant of their surroundings that they had not posted guards. With a smile on his face, Andrew withdrew and as silent as he had come he made his way back.

# 22

Ban Don
30 April 1962
0430 hours

A hand on his shoulder woke Captain Walter and he sat up on his cot, clutching at his weapon.

"What?" he said, his eyes recognizing the figure in front of him.

"Captain Andrew went out about an hour ago, Sir," Lopez said, "and he is not back."

"Shit," Walter said, getting up and putting on his boots. "Did he say where he was going?"

"No, Sir. At first I thought that he was going to the latrine, but when he didn't return I thought I had better let you know."

"Damn it to hell," Walter said, finishing with his boots. "Get the men up Sergeant Lopez, we have to go and find him."

Within minutes the whole team was assembled, weapons checked and ready to go. They went outside and Walter looked at the sky. It was still raining and it was cold. Looking at his watch he noticed the time, almost five in the morning. But there would be no sun this morning, he thought, making the search more difficult.

Where in the hell could Andrew be, he wondered, his stomach tight. He liked the man and respected him and he knew the man could take care of himself, but if something had happened to him while at this place, his Army career would be over.

Okay men, let's go," he said, wrapping a poncho around him.

They started to walk; heading in the general direction that Lopez had seen Andrew the last time, when a shadow materialized from the dark and Andrew Beck walked out of the jungle.

Seeing the group of men together he headed toward them, a smile etched on his face.

"Where in the hell have you been, Andrew?" Walter said, his voice full of concern. "Man, we were ready to go and find you."

"I'm sorry, Captain Walter," Andrew said, "but I didn't have time to wake you before I left."

"What have you been up to?" he asked, seeing the look on Andrew's face.

"I think I found your Viet Cong, Captain Walter," Andrew said. "Not a mile away from here."

Walter looked at him, an incredulous expression on his face and then he said, "You have what?"

"I found your Viet Cong," Andrew repeated, "camped about a mile from here and they have no guards posted."

Walter took the news in stride and he smiled thinking that this was the opportunity that he had been expecting.

"Damn, this is good news," he said, standing next to Andrew. "We can go right now and get them and then they will pay for all the damage they have caused." His eyes smoldered with an inner fire and Andrew thought that he wouldn't want this man for an enemy.

"I suppose you wouldn't want to show me on a map where they are?" he asked, knowing full well what the answer would be.

"Not on your life, Captain," Andrew answered, a smile flickering across his face, "but I'll show you."

Saying that he whirled around and within seconds the Special Forces team and several Montagnards were moving silently through the jungle, the rain helping to dissipate the small amount of noise that they created.

They moved like ghosts, shadows in the night, revenge in their hearts. Slowly they made their way and in less than an hour they had reached the encampment. The rain had finally stopped and the jungle was eerily quiet. Dawn was not far away but darkness still had a hold on the jungle, making everything look distorted.

Reaching the clearing, Walter signaled his men to surround the place and slowly, the Montagnards melted in the jungle. Walter positioned his men silently, making sure that no one was in the line of fire and then he waited. Slowly, second by second, the light intensified until finally Walter could see the forms lying on the ground. One man got up, his black pajama- like clothes, flapping around him, a rifle in his hand. He approached the fire and threw some dry wood on it, squatting next to it, fanning the dying embers. The man got up and looked around. Walking over to another form on the ground and kicking it, he said something that Andrew didn't understand. One by one the men started to get up and Andrew counted fifteen. He was hiding under some brush, next to Walter and he stole a glance toward him. The young man's eyes were glued to the group of men in the clearing, a predatory smile on his face. He saw Walter take a deep breath, uncoiling like a giant snake, his rifle coming up.

"Now," Walter yelled, his carbine spitting fire, the noise rendering the quiet of the jungle. In a second pandemonium erupted, the sound of men engaged in mortal combat filling the air, the cries of wounded and dying men reverberating in the small clearing. Caught in crossfire and completely by surprise, the Viet Cong were unable to put up much of a fight and they fell, the smell of blood and human feces permeating the air. In a matter of seconds Andrew had emptied his carbine and was about to reload when he felt a blow to his shoulder, another to his side, the bullets spinning him around. He gasped at the red hot pain searing his shoulder, his mind reeling and he rolled on the ground coming up on one knee to see a man clad in black running toward him, a demonic look etched deeply on his face. He stumbled to his feet, his left hand searching for the .45 at his waist. He saw the Viet Cong lift his rifle not six feet away from him and he looked death in the face, knowing that there was no way he could reach his pistol before the man fired. And then, the Viet Cong stopped dead in his tracks, a look of consternation spreading on his face and he toppled over, blood gushing from his mouth, half a foot of a blade coming out of his chest. Andrew blinked his eyes, sweat running into them and he sat down hard on the ground. A Montagnard withdrew the knife from the Viet Cong, a smile on his face and then he was gone, searching for more enemies to kill.

Andrew got up slowly, his shoulder and right side on fire and he looked around. Here and there men lay on the jungle floor, the cries of the wounded sending shivers through him. A Special Forces medic looked at the most serious ones, shaking his head and eventually the cries ceased and the clearing was silent once more. Walter searched the fallen men, putting everything that he thought of intelligence value in a rucksack, finally coming over to Andrew. He had two wounded men, nothing serious and one dead Montagnard.

"Man we did good and…" he cut himself off, his eyes glued to Andrew's shoulder.

"Oh shit, you are wounded, damn it," he said, dropping the rucksack on the ground, coming over to inspect the wound, realizing that there were two.

"Medic, medic," he yelled.

"Hell, it's nothing but a scratch," Andrew said, seeing the blood drip on his chest. He sat down feeling lightheaded. The medic came over, ripping off his shirt and working on him to stop the bleeding.

"Take care of him, Jim," Walter said to the medic, getting up and issuing orders.

"Okay men, police the place and let's go."

They picked up the weapons and everything that they thought could be used and with a last look at the clearing they departed, two Montagnards helping Andrew walk, while others carried their dead comrade. Fifteen men lie dead in the clearing, their sightless eyes staring at nothing.

By the time they made it to the outpost Andrew was semi-conscious, the wounds still dripping blood.

"We need to get him out of here," Jim said, bandaging the wound again.

"Right," Walter said, his face showing the concern that he felt seeing his friend like that. "Get on the radio," he said to his RTO, and get the chopper here." His RTO nodded his head in assent, making the call.

Within minutes they had a response and within fifteen minutes several Special Forces had rigged a stretcher with two ponchos, putting Andrew in it. Four men lifted the stretcher and started to walk down the trail, Andrew unconscious now. It took them thirty minutes to arrive and by that time the chopper could be heard. In minutes the bird was down and Andrew was put on board, Walter issuing his orders to the pilot.

"Take him straight to the French Catholic hospital and notify the Embassy." Saying that he looked at Andrew one more time, took off his beret and laid it down on Andrew's chest.

"Take care my friend," he said, his voice almost a whisper.

The chopper lifted slowly, clearing the trees and was gone, Walter standing at the edge of the jungle, his eyes fixed on the bird until it was a speck on the horizon. With a heavy heart he turned around, making his way, his thoughts on the man in the chopper.

# 23

Catholic Hospital
Saigon, South Vietnam
2 May 1962

    Andrew woke up with a bad taste in his mouth and his head splitting. His shoulder was also throbbing and he felt like death warmed over. He tried to sit up and was able to do so after two attempts, the stitches in his side pulling. He swung his legs over the side of the bed and by that time a woman in a nun's habit was at his side.

    "And what do you think you are doing?" she asked in heavily accented English, coming to stand by him.

    "How long have I been here?" he asked.

    "Two days," the nurse said, pushing him gently back on the bed. "You came in in shock and weak from loss of blood."

    "When can I get out?"

    "The doctor is making his rounds, he will be here shortly," she said, giving him a stern look. "Stay in bed."

The nurse left and he closed his eyes. He needed of get out of this place and head for home, he thought. His mind drifting to Captain Walter and the events of the last few days. He was shaken out of his reverie by a hand on his arm and he opened his eyes. A man in the white smock of a doctor was by the bed, a chart in his hand. He was of medium height, balding and his eyes almost black.

'Well Captain Beck, how are you feeling?" he asked, his voice soft, well modulated.

"I'm fine, Sir," Andrew said, "just want to get out of here."

"That's fine with me son," he said, scribbling on the chart. "You seem to be healing well and I can see that you are no stranger to bullet wounds." He paused for a second, closing the chart and then continued, "By the way, my name is Fullbright, Dr. James Fullbright. I'm with the Embassy here in Saigon and was asked to come here and take care of you."

"Nice to meet you, Sir," said Andrew.

This is yours, I presume," he said, pulling a green beret from his pocket. "The chopper pilot said it was."

For a moment he was silent, emotions about to overcome him. "Yes, thank you, Sir," Andrew said, reaching for the beret, seeing the railroad tracks of a captain on it. Walter's beret, Andrew thought. As his eyes moistened, he turned his head away from the doctor.

"You are clear to go as soon as your visitor is through with you."

"Visitor?" Andrew asked, puzzled.

"Yes. There is a Colonel outside wanting to talk with you."

Well, here we go, Andrew thought. Might as well face the music.

Dr. Fullbright looked at him, nodded his head and walked away. In a moment a man came in walking toward the bed and Andrew saw the silver leaf on the shoulder. It was Lt. Colonel Sanders, the military attaché and without preamble, Sanders went at it.

"Captain Beck, consider yourself under house arrest. You have disobeyed a lawful order from a superior officer, creating an embarrassing situation for your government and behaving in a manner unbecoming an officer." He stopped for a second, his face contorted in rage, spittle flying from his lips. "I'll personally forward a letter to General Devlin and I hope he will see fit to court martial you. "You, Captain, are an embarrassment to the Army and the officers corp." He fixed his eyes on Andrew, his eyebrows squinting. "You were also considered AWOL (absent without leave) for the last two weeks. You will depart Saigon at 1800 hours today and report to General Devlin at the Pentagon upon arrival. Now, do I make myself clear, Captain?"

"Yes you do, Colonel," Andrew answered, tired now, thinking that the military attaché was nothing but a paper pusher. What the hell was the man doing in a place like South Vietnam was beyond him. Probably reporting that everything was just fine, Andrew thought, betting that the man had never heard a shot fired in anger in his entire military career.

Colonel Sanders glared at him for a few more seconds and then whirled around, his footsteps loud on the floor.

Well, I guess I'm in trouble, Andrew thought, closing his eyes and drifting off to sleep. Later there would be time to explain and he hoped that General Devlin would be a little more inclined to go with his version than Colonel Sanders'.

# 24

The Pentagon
Washington, DC
7 May 1962

Five days later, he was cooling his heels in the office of the Assistant Chief of Staff waiting for General Devlin to see him. His shoulder was mending well, the pain almost gone now, a twinge only when he used his arm. He had prepared a report in triplicate utilizing a typist from the Pentagon pool when he arrived. His shoulder had been tender and typing was out of the question for him. And here he was now ready to face an ass chewing and whatever Devlin thought was proper for his actions, but hoping the old warrior would understand.

He paced the small office for ten minutes before the secretary came to get him indicating that the General was ready.

"The General will see you now, Sir," she said, opening the door for him.

He went in and saw Devlin at his desk, a major standing by his side. Devlin looked up and a smile came to his face. Andrew stopped in front of the desk, came to attention and saluted. "Captain Beck reporting as ordered, Sir."

Devlin returned the salute and then got up and came around the desk.

"It's good to see you, son," he said, his voice neutral, his eyes fixed on Andrew. "It looks like you had one hell of an interesting trip, Captain. Not only did you piss off the Embassy personnel and the military attaché in Saigon, but you managed to get yourself wounded in action again." He paused for a second, turning to face the other officer in the room. "What do you think about that, Major Goldberg?" he asked, facing Andrew again. Without waiting for an answer he continued, "I have a very interesting letter here from a Colonel Sanders, wanting me to court martial you for dereliction of duty, AWOL, and for disobeying orders." Devlin stopped again coming to stand in front of Andrew while Major Goldberg came to stand on his left side. "Well, Major Beck, what do you have to say in your defense?" General Devlin said. Andrew stood at attention, looking into Devlin's eyes and saw a cold detachment there. Oh hell, I'm in trouble, Andrew thought and then the words of the General finally registered in his brain. Devlin had called him Major, didn't he. He looked at Devlin again and saw the eyes laughing a smile spreading across his face and then the General was laughing, poking him in the chest. Major Goldberg removed the Captain's bars from his shoulder and General Devlin pinned the gold leaf of a major on him.

"Congratulations, son," Devlin said, shaking his hand and then Goldberg was congratulating him too.

"Thank you, Sir," Andrew said, emotions about to overcome him. Here he was expecting a court martial and an ass chewing and now he was being promoted. They sat down to talk, the General eager to hear about Andrew's escapade. Major Goldberg excused himself for a few minutes and when he returned it was with several items in his hands.

General Devlin got up, looking at the papers in Goldberg's hand and then he signaled Andrew to join them.

"Major Beck, here are your orders for the award of the Purple Heart and your authorization for another star on your CIB," Devlin said, handing Andrew the papers. Goldberg passed him a small case and Devlin opened it, taking out the Purple Heart and pinning the medal to Andrew's chest. He was dressed in his class "A" uniform with all his decorations on and it was impressive. Major Goldberg looked at the young Major's chest and he noticed the Medal of Honor, the Legion of Merit, several Purple Hearts and a score of Army commendations, a Bronze Star with a "V" device denoting valor and the CIB and silver wings of a paratrooper. Impressive, very impressive, Goldberg thought, for one so young.

They talked some more and then Goldberg excused himself, leaving the General alone with Major Beck.

"I see you have our report ready," Devlin said, indicating the report that Andrew had prepared.

"Yes sir, it's all there," he said. "I hope it is what you expected."

"Thank you, Andrew," Devlin said, picking up the report. "I'll read it later, but first I would like an overview from you. What do you think about the place?"

Andrew got up, pacing the office, his mind mulling over the question. "From what I've seen, if we get involved in a war in Southeast Asia we would have a hard time fighting a conventional war. Logistics and re-supply issues would be a daunting task due to the terrain and the lack of roads, unless…we used helicopters in great numbers for that. The French went at it for a long time and they found out the hard way, never learning the tactics of the enemy. The smart way for us would be to fight an unconventional war, just like the Vietnamese did before, utilizing the Special Forces like they are now." He stopped, looking at Devlin.

"That's interesting, Andrew." Devlin said, getting up too. "Your ideas and those of some of us, including the President, are the same." He was silent for a few seconds and then he resumed. "But we also have our detractors, Pentagon bureaucrats who think that if we get involved we need to do it with the whole Army and Marines taking part, in other words, a conventional war." They were silent after that, each one lost in their own thoughts. Finally Devlin gave a big sigh and returned to his desk.

"There is no sense worrying about all this," he said, a frown on his face.

"Politics will dictate if we get into a war or not and what kind. It's out of our hands, son."

Devlin punched a button on his phone, getting his secretary. "Get Major Goldberg in here, please."

He waited until the door opened and Goldberg came in.

"I told you that you could have any assignment when you got back," Devlin said, "so what do you want?"

"I would like to go back to Bragg, Sir," Andrew said, "Special Forces."

"Well, Special Forces," Devlin said, a grin flickering across his face. "I thought you might like that." He nodded his head in assent and then continued. "But I must warn you some people think that Special Forces is a dead end, no promotions, no nothing."

"That's all right, Sir," Andrew said. "I don't believe that there is another place that I would rather be if we are going to war."

"That's fine, Andrew. If that is what you want, that's what you will get," Devlin said. "I'll have Major Goldberg cut your orders and you can go to Bragg tomorrow. Anything else I can do for you?"

Andrew thought about that for a second and then he smiled.

"There is a friend, Sir, Sgt. Ragsdale. I would appreciate it if he could be assigned with me."

"No problem about that, Andrew," Devlin said. "The way I understand it they are looking for qualified men to join them. Give Major Goldberg his name, rank and serial number and he will be reassigned to Bragg."

Devlin walked toward Andrew, extending his hand, a fond look in his eyes. "Take care, son, and God speed," he said.

Andrew shook his hand and then came to attention, saluting the General. Devlin returned it and Andrew did an about face and was gone, leaving Devlin immersed in his thoughts.

# 25

U.S. Army Special Warfare School
Fort Bragg, North Carolina
8 May 1962

    Brigadier General Raymond Ashley Brown, commanding officer, U.S. Army Special Warfare School, was sitting at his desk going over the manpower requisitions and the status of his command when there was a light knock at the door and Sgt. Major Cunningham stepped in.

    "There is a Major outside, Sir," Cunningham said, coming to attention in front of the desk, "said he is reporting in."

    General Brown's eyebrow went up in a silent question and he looked at Sgt. Major Cunningham.

    "Reporting?" he asked finally. Special Forces didn't get very many field officers unless they were "problem" officers that somebody was trying hard to get rid off, especially a Major, and General Brown wondered what he was getting now.

    "Yes Sir, that's what he said."

    "Well, Sgt. Major, tell him to step in please."

Cunningham exited the office and seconds later a Major in class "A" uniform stepped in, stopping three feet in front of the desk, coming to attention, delivering a crisp parade perfect salute.

"Sir, Major Beck, reporting for duty, Sir."

General Brown returned the salute and for a few moments he was silent, his eyes measuring the officer in front of him. He saw a tall handsome looking man, every inch the soldier and he was pleased. And then his eyes fastened on the man's chest and he did a double take. The man in front of him had a ribbon, blue in color, five stars on it and he recognized the Medal of Honor. He continued to look, noticing the Purple Heart, bronze oak leaf cluster showing several awards, a Legion of Merit, Bronze Star with "V" device and several more medals on the man's chest. He saw the silver wings of a paratrooper and the CIB with a star, meaning a second award and he was duly impressed. Most of the medals and badges on the soldier's chest were, without a doubt, hard won and there weren't that many Medal of Honor winners around. You have to earn that one, he thought, they don't just give those away lightly. Damn, but this man is a soldier, he thought again, wondering what he had done right for the Gods to smile upon him like that now. He had good-quality soldiers, he knew that, but men of this caliber were few and far between in the Army Special Forces. He had busted his chops asking for men like this one, and had lost more times than he cared to admit. The good ones apparently thought of Special Forces as a passing fad, not something that was going to be around much longer.

He came around the desk, extending his hand, fixing his eyes on the man and he smiled.

"Glad to have you with us, Major," General Brown said, shaking hands. "Sit down, if you please."

They sat down and Sgt. Major Cunningham came in as if on cue.

"Would you like some refreshment or coffee?" Brown asked.

"Coffee would be fine, Sir."

"Coffee all around, please Charlie," General Brown said.

Sgt. Major nodded his head and departed, leaving them alone.

"May I see a copy of your orders, Major?"

Andrew opened the brief case and extracted some papers, handing them over to General Brown.

"I see that you have a copy of your 201 file, Major Beck," Brown said. "May I see it also, please?"

Andrew complied with the request and handed over the file, watching the General begin to read.

He sat quietly waiting, his eyes taking in the General. Brown was a ruddy-faced man, his head almost bald. His eyes were hazel, clear and intelligent. He had a wide forehead and a long face with a strong jaw line.

Cunningham came in with a tray of coffee, sugar and cream on it and set it down, handing the General a mug.

"Your coffee, Sir," Cunningham said.

Brown grunted something, reaching over, his eyes still glued to the file. He put the mug down, continuing his reading, oblivious to Andrew and Cunningham who were sitting now, sipping their coffee. From time to time General Brown raised his eyebrows, like a man reading something interesting and on more than one occasion his eyes fixed on Andrew for a few seconds, giving him a speculative look.

He finally finished reading, dropping the file on the coffee table.

"To tell you that I'm impressed is not the half of it, son," he said, sipping his coffee, a smile crossing his face.

"Thank you, Sir," Andrew said, his face reddening.

"So you are the one, huh?" he asked, a mischievous glint in his eyes and Andrew was baffled by the question.

"I beg your pardon, General, but I don't know what you are referring to."

General Brown got up pacing the office, his eyes laughing.

"Sgt. Major, this young man in here is the one," he said, his voice strong, chuckling. "He is the one we heard about, the one with Richard Walter in Vietnam."

"I'll be damned," Cunningham said, surprise registering in his eyes and then realizing that he had cursed in front of the commanding General, "Begging your pardon, Sir."

General Brown made a dismissive gesture with his hand and continued.

"We heard about you, Major, from your friend Captain Walter," he said, coming back and sitting down again. "He holds you in the greatest regard, singing your praises. And now you are here."

"Yes, Sir," Andrew said, surprised at the fact that his exploits were common knowledge here. "Major General Devlin was gracious enough to offer me my choice of assignments when I got back from my trip and I chose this."

"Ah, Devlin. Yes, he is a friend," General Brown said, standing up. "Well Major Beck, we are happy to have you here and I hope that you find this to your liking. We pride ourselves in being the best there is in the Army and you certainly qualify for the job. You will be assigned to the Officer's Qualification Course and after that we will see what we can get you."

The interview was over and Andrew got up, coming to attention, saluting.

Brown returned the salute saying, "Sgt. Major Cunningham will see to your quarters. Give him your orders and he will get you through personnel. He extended his hand and said, "It's good to have you with us, Major."

"Thank you, Sir," Andrew said, exiting the office, thinking that he had made the right decision about Special Forces.

A few days later while he was still getting oriented he received a call from Sgt. Major Cunningham.

"Major, there is this gorilla in my office, a Sgt. First Class, saying that he is a friend of yours and that you are responsible for him being here." He paused for a second and then came back on the line. "He said his name is Paul Ragsdale."

Andrew laughed, hearing the news. "Yes, he is an old friend, Sgt. Major. He is a good man and I believe that we could use him at Special Forces. Take care of him, will you?"

"Yes, Sir, if you say so, Major." Cunningham said, laughter in his voice.

And then the training started. For the next six months they went through the most extensive physically demanding training they had ever seen. From weapons to medicine to operations and intelligence, they went through it. There was military free-fall parachuting or HALO (high altitude low opening) and cross training in different skills. After that it was language school for Andrew, specializing in Vietnamese and then he was ready for a command.

By the time they had graduated the number of Special Forces advisors in Vietnam had increased steadily, training the South Vietnamese in the art of counterinsurgency, molding the various tribes into a credible anti-Communist force. By the middle of 1963, Andrew and Paul were on their way to South Vietnam, Andrew as a Detachment Commander and Paul as weapons expert of an A-team, ready to face the challenges of a new war, and a new way of fighting. The jungles of Vietnam were far away from the frozen grounds of Korea, but to Andrew it was just part of being a soldier and part of his duty. His experience and devotion to duty helped him to face the dangers of a hostile environment with honor and dedication, doing his best to save lives, looking after the welfare of his men, leading by example and slowly, the legend grew. The men of the Green Beret earned their reputation in far away places, with exotic sounding names like Am Dong, Song Zoo and a hundred others. While they fought and bled and sacrificed at the side of the hundreds of friendly natives who composed their outposts, they fought a war to win the minds, the friendship and hearts of the civilian population. For Andrew, Vietnam was the last line, the place to stop communism and he threw himself into the conflict with heart, mind and soul. Little did he know that it would also be the place of his greatest achievement and the end of his life.

# 26

U.S. Army Special Warfare School
Fort Bragg, North Carolina
Housing Area
December 1964

    Andrew Beck lit a cigarette and stretched his long legs, savoring the smoke. He had tried several times to quit the damn things, but had started back soon after quitting. He had resigned himself to the fact that some things were better left alone and this was one of them.

    Paul Ragsdale was sitting next to him on the porch, enjoying one of his nasty cigars, watching the watery sun setting. It was cold in Bragg, Christmas night and the two friends were sharing the evening. They had returned from Vietnam a few weeks ago and had taken leave together, thirty days that they promised would be unforgettable. They both were dark, their skin tanned to a golden hue, Paul's hair bleached almost white by the tropical sun of Vietnam

    Lynn was in the house getting ready for an evening out and Paul had been trying hard to get Andrew to go with them.

"No sir, no way," Andrew said for the tenth time, shaking his head to emphasize the point. "I'm not going anywhere."

"Oh hell, come on man, there is no sense in you staying here all by yourself," Paul said again. "We can get a baby sitter and you can come with us."

"You go, my friend," Andrew said, a note of finality in his voice. At that moment Lynn came out and the two men got up, Paul looking at his wife with admiration. After one child she was still holding her figure and looking good.

"Well, how do I look?" she asked, twirling around for them. She was dressed in tight black pants and a black sweater, her golden hair cascading down her back, a single strand of pearls around her throat.

Paul whistled and Lynn smiled, while Andrew nodded his head in assent, a smile flickering across his face. He stood still watching the woman in front of him, and his mind went back to a beautiful girl, a happy smile on her face and he thought of Catherine, wondering how the years had dealt with her. A far away look came into his gray-green eyes and something wet touched his cheek. He shook his head, clearing his mind, embarrassed at his weakness and looked around to see his friend staring at him in puzzlement, Lynn looking at both of them.

"Are you okay?" Paul asked, concern in his voice.

"Yes, I'm fine," Andrew said, forcing a smile to his face. "You both go on. I'll have a great time baby-sitting for that monster inside."

"That monster is your godchild, mister," Lynn said, smiling outside, but her heart breaking. She was a woman with a woman's intuition and she knew what was bothering Andrew Beck. Underneath the self-control and the image of toughness, there was a broken heart in pain, still in love with the woman who had shattered it. Maybe the years had assuaged the pain, but it was still there.

Paul stared at his friend for a second longer and then whirled around, taking Lynn by the arm and pushing her gently.

Andrew saw them go and went inside, listening intently for any noise coming from the baby's room. Caroline was two years old, the image of her mother and Andrew had become the godfather when she was born.

There was no noise from the room and Andrew sat down, a drink in his hand, the TV on. He sipped the drink slowly, his mind a jumble of thoughts, mostly about Catherine and then he closed his eyes, the perfect figure of the woman that he loved coming to him. Why had she lied to him?, he wondered for the thousandth time; why had she gone and married someone without having the decency to let him know?. Was it all a lie, the words of love, the lovemaking? On and on it went, until Andrew couldn't stand it any longer and he got up, mad at himself for his weakness.

He paced the floor of the small living room, finishing his drink, fixing another. He was tired, the prospect of another lonely Christmas night weighing heavily on his mind. He had another week before his leave was over and he and Paul would report for duty again.

He sat down again, watching the images on the TV, sipping his drink, and refusing to let his mind dwell on Catherine any more. He sat there, his brain numb, until the cry of a small child brought him out of his reverie and he got up. Duty called, he thought, smiling ruefully he headed for the child's room, the memories of long ago still haunting him.

# 27

U.S. Army Special Warfare School
Fort Bragg, North Carolina
January 1965

    Andrew Beck and General Brown were sitting in his office, sharing a drink, and enjoying a respite from their daily routine. Brown sipped his drink, looking at Andrew and he said, "How would you like to go back to Nam, Andrew?"

    Andrew fixed his eyes on the General, wondering what the old man had in store for him now.

    "When?" he asked.

    "In about a week," Brown said, getting up and shuffling some papers on his desk until he found what he was looking for. "As you know, we established a provisional headquarters for the 5th Group in Nha Trang back in September 1964, and now we have received the go ahead to make it permanent." He handed Andrew a file, sitting down again. "I need for you to go over this and make sure that all the specifications are followed to the letter and get the place running right. Everything you need to know is there and we will support you with everything you need." He stopped talking and finished his drink. "I know you just got back but I think you are the man I need for this operation. The 5th Group will have full responsibility for Vietnam from now on."

Andrew flipped through the pages, his mind reaching a decision. Why not, he thought. War is what I do best and there is nothing to hold me here anyway. He heard himself talking, saying yes he would go and then he was out of the office, making preparations to go. A week later he was back in Vietnam, the smell of the country now familiar in his nostrils. This time Paul stayed behind, much to his chagrin, Andrew making sure that he spent time at Bragg, close to his family. Lynn had announced that she was pregnant again and Andrew wanted to make sure that Paul was around for the baby.

By February 1965, Nha Trang had become the 5th Special Forces Group's permanent headquarters and then, in March 1965, President Lyndon B. Johnson committed the first conventional war units to Vietnam. First came the Marines, landing at Da Nang and then, in June, the 173rd Airborne Brigade of the Army entered the conflict. Things heated up pretty fast after that and the body bags started to come home, Vietnam turned into what Andrew had feared it would be, a quagmire with no end in sight.

By the end of 1965, Andrew had returned home, becoming the S-3 for the school, planning operations and honing his skills as a commander, taking a respite from the war that raged across Southeast Asia. Then, in 1968, the same day that Andrew Beck received his promotion to Lt. Colonel, the North attacked South Vietnam in what was called the Tet Offensive, the New Year's holiday. The American public went crazy, losing their faith in the government, demonstrations and riots erupting everywhere until the Johnson administration was reduced to nothing, unable to win the war, unable to disengage from the quicksand that was Vietnam. For Andrew it was painful to see his beloved country torn apart by the war and the protesters, baffled by the incredible stupidity of the demonstrations. Didn't they realize that the more they protested the more GIs would die in the fields of Vietnam? That instead of trying to come to the conference table they would keep up the struggle, thinking that the American people would win the war for them? As far as Andrew was concerned all the demonstrations and talk from celebrities about the war only helped the resolve of the Communists and made matters worse in Vietnam for our soldiers. That was treason, pure and simple, and all it did was weaken the United States.

By 1969 Richard Nixon had taken office and slowly the United States began a withdrawal from Vietnam. Gradually Andrew saw the Special Forces camps turned over to South Vietnam and finally only a handful of teams remained in Vietnam, launching secret missions. By 1972 the Special Forces role in Vietnam was pretty much over and Andrew thought the war would be finished soon. And then, lady luck quit smiling on him.

U. S. Army JFK Special Warfare School
Office of the Commanding General
10 December 1972

General Taylor picked up the phone and dialed, his secretary answering immediately. "Get Colonel Beck in here, please," he said, hanging up the phone. Taylor was a beefy man, slightly overweight with a receding hairline. He had become the commanding General six months before and in that time had learned to appreciate the good fortune that he had in Colonel Beck, his S-1, in charged of intelligence. And now he needed him. Besides the General there was a man in civilian clothes in his office and another officer from the office of the Chief of Special Operations at the Pentagon. For the last two hours they had been immersed in a top-secret conversation concerning the fate of one man. Papers and pictures were strung all over the coffee table, along with the remnants of sandwiches and coffee cups. The civilian was a tall man, broad shouldered, with short brown hair. His eyes were brown in color and they didn't miss anything. He was CIA and had come in early in the morning requesting a meeting with the General, accompanied by the Colonel from the Pentagon.

General Taylor sat down next to the two other men and they waited in silence for Colonel Beck to come in. A few seconds later there was a knock on the door and Lt. Colonel Andrew Beck came in, snapping to attention and reporting to the General.

"Sir, Lt. Colonel Beck reporting, Sir."

"At ease, Beck," General Taylor said. "Sit down."

Andrew did as he was asked and then his gaze drifted around the room. He saw the civilian man and guessed correctly that he was CIA and he noticed the Colonel from the Pentagon.

"Gentlemen, this is Colonel Beck, the officer I have been telling you about," Taylor said. Both men nodded their heads; their eyes fixed on Andrew. The civilian man had a file in his hand and was reading, his eyes drifting to Andrew on occasion. Andrew glanced at the file and he could swear that it was his 201 file. The General offered coffee and Andrew accepted, knowing that something was brewing and that General Taylor was not pleased with it. The coffee came and Andrew settled down to wait.

He sipped his coffee, enjoying the strong brew and then the civilian man said, "Are you familiar with the Loc Ninh area?"

Andrew nodded his head in assent, his eyes fixed on the man.

The CIA agent got up, apparently his mind made up and then he continued asking questions. It wasn't long before Andrew realized that they were planning a mission in Vietnam and the CIA was in charge. Finally the man came straight to the point, addressing Andrew.

"In two weeks this man will be in the area specified and we have orders to sanction the individual, Colonel. The subject in question is very high in the North Vietnamese hierarchy and if we can eliminate him it would help the South tremendously. This is a secret mission and it was suggested by General Taylor that you would be the best man to attempt it." He picked up a photograph from the coffee table and handed it to Andrew. The face of a Vietnamese General looked back at him, the almond shaped eyes intelligent and penetrating. He turned the photo around and read the caption on the back—General Von Giap. There was a date and a signature and nothing else. Andrew put it down and his eyes fastened on the CIA man again.

For the next three hours they planned the mission, checking the ins and outs and the degree of difficulty that it represented. Andrew knew the area well and the last report they had about it was that the North Vietnamese army heavily patrolled it. Finally, late that evening, the plan was approved and Andrew found himself in charge of another mission to Vietnam.   Leaving the office he started his preparations, picking his men carefully, determining the base of operations and the resources that he would need to carry out the mission successfully. He had no plans to take Paul Ragsdale with him, but when Paul heard that he was asking for volunteers for a mission there was no way that he could turn him down and finally his name was added to the list. The members of the A-Team started leaving the next day, heading for a secret base in Thailand. They would regroup there, arriving in Vietnam a couple of days before the hit, send some reconnaissance teams to gather intelligence and with luck, accomplish the mission.

# 28

U.S. Army Special Warfare School
Fort Bragg, North Carolina
14 December 1972

Andrew beck was finishing his packing when the phone in his office rang. He had a plane to catch at Pope Air Force Base in about an hour, heading for Washington, DC and he was running late. He picked up the phone listening to the familiar voice of the Sgt. Major.

"Sir, you have a call waiting on the other line."

"Thanks, Cunningham," he said. He took the call and once again his world was turned upside down.

"Colonel Beck speaking," he said.

"Well, Colonel Beck, I wondered if you remembered me, Sir," the voice on the other end of the line said and Andrew's stomach fluttered. The voice was accented and familiar. And then he had it—Lt. Henry Weatherly, Catherine's brother.

Memories came flooding back and for a second he thought about hanging up the phone. But the moment passed and he waited.

"This is Henry Weatherly, Catherine's brother and I would like very much to speak with you."

Andrew listened to the voice of the past and he shuddered, his mind running wild. "What is it that you want Mr. Weatherly?" he asked, none too pleasant.

"Andrew, I know that you probably feel that Catherine played with your feelings and that she betrayed you," Weatherly said, "but I promise you that if you let me explain you will understand her actions. Something happened and there are things that you need to know Andrew, so I ask you to come to Boston and meet with me."

Andrew thought about the request. There was something in Henry Weatherly's voice that caught his attention.

"What is going on, Henry?" he asked, his heart beating fast now.

"I can't talk about such matters on the phone, Andrew," he said, "but if you could come, I promise you will not regret it."

Andrew thought about it for a moment, coming to the conclusion that he didn't have anything to lose by talking to Henry Weatherly.

"Okay, I'll come, Henry. I have to catch a plane in a few minutes for Washington and I can see you tomorrow morning."

"That is great," Henry Weatherly said and then he gave the address of his office, setting a meeting for nine the next morning. Andrew hung up wondering what that was all about and picked up his bag, exiting the office. An hour later he was on his way. There would be another meeting at the Pentagon and the next day he would be on his way to Vietnam, hopefully for the last time. But first he would have his meeting with Henry Weatherly and find out what was so important that Weatherly had bothered to search for him with such diligence.

# 29

Boston, Massachusetts
15 December 1972

    Andrew Beck arrived early at the office of Henry Weatherly. When he announced his name the secretary ushered him into an extremely elegant office and asked if he would care for breakfast. Andrew settled for black coffee, and in seconds a silver tray was brought in with coffee and pastries. He glanced around the office, his eyes taking in the plaque on the wall, the Silver Star and the Purple Heart and he read the citation, approval in his eyes. He fixed his coffee and was sipping it when the door opened and Henry Weatherly came in, his limp clearly visible. He came straight to Andrew and shook his hand affectionately, thinking that the years had been kind to Andrew Beck.

    "How are you, Andrew," he said, his eyes taking in the man in uniform, the incredible number of ribbons on his chest, the blue ribbon with the five white stars that he knew was the Medal of Honor. Andrew was in his class "A" uniform, the Green Beret on his head and he looked every inch the soldier. "Sorry to keep you waiting."

Andrew waived his hand in a dismissive gesture, following Henry Weatherly with his eyes. "I'm fine, Henry," Andrew said, noticing the man's limp. Henry saw the direction of his eyes and he said, patting his leg, "A gift from Korea, nothing much." He came around his desk, sitting down and facing Andrew. "Sit down, please. I believe that what I have to tell you would be better received if you are sitting."

Andrew did as he was asked, raising an eyebrow in question. Henry Weatherly fastened his eyes on Andrew, took a deep breath and slowly, started talking. For the next thirty minutes he talked while Andrew's face registered every word and every bit of news that Henry Weatherly threw at him. He remained quiet, his mind in turmoil. When Henry Weatherly told him about Catherine's death a hollow sound escaped his lips and his heart twisted in pain. And then came the news of a son and Andrew Beck felt his head spin, his breath came short, until everything was a blur and he thought his heart would explode with the emotions. All these years he had thought that Catherine had lied to him, that she had but used him and now he understood the reason for her silence and the part that her father had played. And she was dead, Andrew thought, every fiber of his body rebelling at the thought. And I have a son, almost grown he thought again, his mind marveling at the notion.

After Henry finished there was silence, finally broken by Andrew.

"Tell me about my son," he said, his voice sounding strange to his ears.

"His name is Craig and he is a very handsome young man," Henry said, talking affectionately about the boy. It was obvious that Henry loved the boy and thought the world of him.

"As a matter of fact…" Henry cut himself off, getting up and approaching a small table at the corner of the office. Several pictures were there and he picked one up, bringing it back to Andrew.

Andrew took it from him and looked at the face. Damn, but if the boy looked just like him, Andrew thought, noticing the black, curly hair and the eyes. He nodded his head in approval and handed it back. Henry Weatherly shook his head and said, "You can keep it, Andrew."

"Thank you, Henry, I appreciate that," he said, his hand removing the picture from the frame and putting it in his breast pocket.

Henry saw him, and his heart filled with pity. He knew the man in front of him was suffering and that he had loved his sister dearly all these years. At that moment he made up his mind.

"Your son is receiving an award today from Harvard, Andrew. In about an hour there will be a ceremony honoring the Athletic Department and he will be there. If you want to you can come and see him."

Andrew fixed his eyes on Henry Weatherly and saw the expression on the man's face. His heart was still racing, his mind a jumble of thoughts, emotions running wild.

"Thank you, Henry," he said softly, "I would like that very much."

With Henry driving they made their way to the imposing building that was Harvard Alumni Center and they entered. The ceremony had already started and they sat in silence. At one point Henry pointed at a young man going up to the front, but he was too far away from them for Andrew to get a good look. The ceremony was over shortly after that and while Henry and Andrew talked, a young man made his way toward them. Andrew noticed him and his heart started beating hard again. It was his son, the looks unmistakable. He was a tall man, like his father, the same eyes and hair, except longer. He had a long, handsome face, showing a happy smile now and when he stopped next to them, his eyes looked at the stranger with frank curiosity.

"Hi, Uncle Henry," he said, smiling fondly at the man. Henry cleared his throat and looked at Andrew. The man was obviously controlling himself with an incredible effort.

"Congratulations, son," Henry said, embracing the young man. "This is a friend of mine, Colonel Beck." And then, "Andrew, this is my nephew, Craig Barlow."

Andrew extended his hand, feeling the strong grip of the young man as he returned the shake.

"Nice to meet you, son," he said, "and congratulations."

"Nice meeting you too, Sir," Craig Barlow said, his eyes fastened on the man's face. For some strange reason he thought he knew the man in front of him, but then he shook his head slightly. He had never seen the man, he was sure of that. Still, the sense that he was connected to him somehow stayed with him until the man finally shook his hand again, saying his goodbye. Andrew extended his hand and looked at Craig and for a moment Craig thought there was something wrong with him, his body shaking with the force of some concealed emotion. Craig looked into the man's eyes and he saw an incredible yearning and pain. Pain so real that young Craig Barlow had a feeling that something of tremendous importance was going on. But then the man shook his head, saying goodbye to Henry Weatherly and with a last look at Craig, put a Green Beret on his head and walked away leaving Craig Barlow in confusion, feeling like he had lost something incredibly close to him.

# 30

Loc Nihn Province
Republic of Vietnam
25 December 1972
1000 hours

    Andrew Beck paced the small hut that served as a Forward Operating Base in Loc Nihn, monitoring the radio. Operation 'Pegasus', the code name used for the mission has been underway for more than ten hours and communications had been sporadic at best. The A-Team had been inserted by helicopter in a dense jungle area east of Loc Nihn, where the target was supposed to show early in the morning. It was now ten in the morning and no news from the team. They were late, and if the hit had not taken place by now they needed to abort. The damn place was crawling with North Vietnamese troops and every minute that they stayed in place increased the chance that they would be discovered. Andrew looked up at the sky, noticing the dark angry clouds rolling by. The weather was getting nasty, and he could smell rain in the air. His spirit was still buoyant after learning that he had a son and meeting him, if briefly and he had told Paul everything, sharing with him all the news that he had obtained from Henry Weatherly.

He lit a cigarette with his gold lighter, his instincts telling him that something was about to go haywire with the mission and he hoped that he was wrong. But he wasn't.

And then, it happened. In the quiet of the hut the sound emanating from the radio was startling, making everyone jump. Amid the sound of small arms fire, the agitated voice of the team commander could be heard.

"Green One, Green One, this is Alpha Leader, get us out, get us out!"

Andrew heard the cry and he ran to the radio, his heart in his mouth.

Anxiously, he waited for more words, but the radio was silent and all efforts by the RTO to raise the A-Team were unsuccessful. Upon hearing the words another RTO had immediately called the extraction helicopter that Andrew had placed on standby and fifteen minutes later the lead pilot could be heard.

"Green One, this is a hot LZ," I repeat, this is a hot LZ. Unable to extract." Ten minutes later the extraction helicopters were back, empty handed, the birds riddled with holes, several crewmembers wounded, one chopper trailing black smoke. Andrew ran outside, his eyes taking in the stricken helicopters and the wounded being off-loaded. Running to the nearest pilot he checked with him confirming that the bird was ready to go and he jumped in, directing the pilot to take off. Paul was in danger, maybe dead by now and he sure as hell was not going to sit idle while his best friend was in a dire predicament. While in the chopper he contacted the support elements, making sure that gunships were heading in the general direction where the Team was located and that artillery was ready to go as soon as he could get them a fix. While in the chopper he tried to establish contact with the Team and finally was rewarded. "Green One this is Alpha, one niner zero, requesting emergency reinforcements and Med-Evac." Andrew listened to the transmission and he could swear that the voice on the radio was Paul's.

With a lump in his throat he answered, willing the chopper to fly faster. "Alpha one niner zero, Green One reads you loud and clear. Hang on, we're coming." Reaching the location Andrew looked out, trying to catch a glimpse of the beleaguered Team, but the jungle covering was too dense. He strapped a radio to his back and snatched several magazines of ammo and his CAR-15. Directing the bird to a clearing he ordered the pilot to get lower and immediately the sound of small arms fire could be heard. Fifteen feet from the ground he jumped, rolling around on the ground, coming up just in time to see an enemy soldier firing an RPG (Rifle propelled grenade) and striking the nose of the chopper. He aimed his CAR-15, letting loose in full automatic fire and saw the bullets strike the man in the chest, the impact bowling him over. At the same time there was a loud explosion and he looked up to see the chopper careening downward, the nose of the aircraft completely gone, flames and smoke billowing in the air. With a tremendous crash the bird went down, tearing itself apart on the ground, Andrew rushing toward it, attempting to pull out the crew. With a glance he realized that the pilot and co-pilot were dead, and the door gunner was seriously injured. He grabbed the man with one hand, his eyes searching the edge of the jungle, bullets striking the burning chopper. Overhead he could hear the sound of the gunships firing and all around him was the cacophony of small arms fire and anti-aircraft guns going off. Something hit him on his back and he staggered, going down, feeling the wetness running down his back.

He put the wounded soldier down, snatching the radio. He looked around listening to the sound of AK-47s, M-16s and the M-60 machine guns from the helicopters and suddenly the air was rendered by the sound of mortars exploding, red-hot fragments peppering the downed chopper, striking his legs. The bastards had put a short fuse on the mortar rounds, Andrew thought, making them explode at tree level. He felt wetness on his face and realized that it was raining. The flames had gone out on the chopper, black smoke still rising and he dragged the wounded soldier to it, the dense smoke camouflaging his actions. His left shoulder was painful to move and when he looked at the radio he noticed that a bullet had ricocheted from it, hitting his shoulder. Guiding himself by the sound of M-16 firing, he was finally able to locate the Team and rushed to them, bullets searched for him like crazy hornets. Someone's still alive, Andrew thought, hearing the firing of the M-16 increased when he sprinted for the Team. He reached them and the first person he recognized was Paul, a smile on his face the camouflaged paint making him look alien. "I knew you would come," he said above the infernal noise surrounding them. Andrew smiled back and then he was busy, checking the dead and wounded, directing the survivors to place their fire around the edge of the jungle. Out of a twelve-man team, three were dead, including the team commander and most of the others were wounded, including Paul, a nasty red gash on his face. The medic was helping the worst cases, working feverishly on them. They were lying on the ground with hardly any cover and Andrew realized that they would be overrun in no time if they stayed there much longer. The enemy was all around them, keeping low, biding their time.

Seeing the bad position they were in Andrew decided to move the team and inching closer to Paul he yelled close to his ear.

"We have to move, get the men ready to go." Paul nodded his head, firing like a maniac at anything that moved. Andrew tapped the first man on the shoulder and they both took off at a dead run, Andrew assisting the wounded man, the rest of the team covering as best they could. They covered the short distance in seconds and Andrew dropped the man by the chopper next to the other wounded GI. He ran back and just before reaching the team he was wounded again, this time in the leg and arm. Despite that, he pulled one man over his shoulder and assisting another one he yelled at Paul to come on. Paul jumped up, reaching for one of his comrades and started following Andrew. They made it under an incredible volume of small arms fire directed at them, reaching the downed chopper. Andrew directed the men to fire into the jungle, facilitating the removal of the other wounded soldiers and one more time he returned. His head was spinning, his breath coming in ragged gasps, his chest burning and the wounds on his legs were beginning to impede his running. He shook his head to clear away the pain and with an effort continued his running, reaching the team members again. Despite his wounds Andrew herded the rest of the men, five in all, and covering their retreat with automatic fire they rushed to the downed chopper. When everyone was finally there Andrew got on the radio and giving their fix, he called for artillery and gunships. Using the chopper for cover Andrew directed the Med-Evac to land, popping green smoke when he heard the rotors approaching. Seeing the chopper coming down he started to get up when he saw movement from the corner of his eyes. He whirled around, the rain and the wind thrown about from the swirling blades of the Huey impeding his vision. He wiped his face and felt himself being pushed roughly by a hand and then, Paul was there, his rifle spitting fire, his face contorted in rage. He looked around, confused, seeing the lifeless form of two enemy soldiers wreathing on the ground, so close that there would not have been any way he could have stopped them. Realizing that his friend had saved his life he turned, his eyes fastened on the man on the ground. Paul was down, his hands clutching his stomach, blood gushing from the wound. With a cry of pure rage, Andrew ran to him, pulling his head up. "Medic, medic," he yelled, wiping his friend's face, seeing the eyes open, the pain contorting his features. The medic came, pushing him roughly out of the way, working to stop the bleeding.

Andrew got up, his brain registering the fact that the enemy was still there, intent on exterminating them all. While the Med-Evac picked up the wounded, another Huey was disgorging a load of Special Forces, while the Cobra gunships covered every inch of ground that was exposed, trying their best to keep the heads of the enemy force down long enough for the choppers to do their job. Artillery was coming in now, the explosions reverberating all around them. Grenades started coming in, fragments hitting Andrew on the chest and face and he went down again, the pain incredibly sharp, his mind in agony. For a second he lay there, absorbing the intense pain and then, one more time, he got up, his indomitable will pushing him to the limits. There were three dead men lying on the ground and Andrew was not about to leave them there. He reached the spot and hurriedly searched the dead team leader for any secret documents. He picked up the man, staggering and moved back to the small defensive perimeter by the chopper. Laying the man down he returned again, finally getting everyone back. He was putting the last man down when a powerful blow to his chest made him stagger backwards. He went down on one knee, his CAR-15 coming up and he fired at the figure of the enemy soldier rushing him, the bullets hitting the face, disintegrating it. He fell down next to the chopper, feeling a hand reach for him and he looked into the eyes of his friend, Paul. He coughed, blood spilling out of his mouth, heard Paul calling for help and his hand reached for his shirt pocket. A gentle rain was coming down, mixing with the blood on his face and he felt an incredible numbness spreading all over him. Oh my God, I'm dying, he thought, his mind refusing to acknowledge the truth, the incredible pain eating at him. I don't want to die, God, I don't want to die. Not now, not now, his mind screamed inside, his body thrashing on the jungle floor. And it was cold, oh so cold, Andrew thought, his eyes closing, his mind bringing forward the face of a young man, smiling, his eyes full of life and wonderment. And suddenly there was peace. His whole body relaxed and a smile spread over his face. His hand finally reached his pocket and he pulled out the picture of his son, his clouded eyes barely able to see the handsome face, blood and mud smearing the glossy print.

"Paul, Paul," he said, feeling an unbearable pressure on his chest, unable to breath. "Tell my son... tell him that I..." he never finished. His head came up and his face registered something like wonder and then he let go. Andrew Beck died, his gray-green eyes staring at nothing, the life that had shown so strong in them now extinguished. Paul Ragsdale crawled toward his friend, reaching over with an incredible effort to cradle his head, silent tears running down his face, mixing with the blood and the rain.

More choppers came in bringing more reinforcements and medics and finally, all the wounded men were loaded and the choppers lifted up, the sound of the firefight below diminishing. Paul Ragsdale looked at the face of his friend and gently closed his eyes. He plucked the blood-smeared picture of the young man that was Andrew's son from his cold hands and put it away. He stared at the jungle below, his heart cold, his eyes incredibly sad, his powerful arms rocking gently the body of the man who had been more like a brother to him and felt a part of him slowly die that day.

# 31

Part III
The Medal
Fort Brag, North Carolina
10 May 1973

    The first hint of daylight was showing up in the sky when Paul Ragsdale got up from the chair that he had been sitting in for most of the night and silently wiped the tears from his eyes. They had been talking all night, the hours flying by, engrossed in the story that was told. Paul looked at Craig and saw the wetness in the young man's eyes and he looked away. He went in the house, leaving Craig alone, coming back several minutes later with two cups of coffee and a wooden box. This early in the morning it was cool and Craig reached for the coffee with delight. He sipped the hot brew, his mind feeling numb with all the things he had learned about not just his father, but also about his mother. He shook his head, getting up and pacing the small porch, watching the sun finally breaking over the horizon, daylight spreading over the land.

Paul watched him silently for a few minutes and then he said, "This is yours," putting the wooden box on the picnic table. "I have to get ready for work, so take your time," he said gently, getting up and going into the house.

Craig looked at the box, observing the exquisite finish of the wood, the hand carved dragon on the lid and he reached for it. It was about two feet long by one and a half feet wide and heavy. He opened the box, noticing the inside covered with a purple felt cloth, his eyes taking in the contents. There was a gold cigarette lighter and some papers, letters and money and several medals and badges. He recognized the Purple Heart, the CIB and the Parachute Wings and then, his eyes saw the blue sash and he knew he was looking at the Medal of Honor. He picked it up, looking at the inscription and his heart beat faster, the medal beautiful in its simplicity and meaning. He put the box down, his fingers rummaging through the papers, noticing the insurance policies and other odds and ends and then he saw the picture. He picked it up, bringing it closer to his face, thinking that it was his father. There was something smeared over the face of the man, dirt and something else and he wet his finger, cleaning off the face. It was then that he realized that he was the man in the picture and that the dirt was mixed with blood and his throat constricted, a painful lump threatened to choke him. The blood of my father, he thought.

"Oh my lord...oh Lord," he said softly, tears streaming down his face, the sobs coming out in a wrenching, painful sound. How long he stood there he didn't know, but finally the sound of voices in the house brought him out of it and he closed the box, taking a deep breath to clear his head. He walked inside, finding Paul and Lynn at the breakfast table.

"Want some breakfast?" Paul asked, his eyes taking in the state the young man was in. It was too much too fast, Paul thought. The young man had gone through a lot in a few short hours.

"No…no thanks," Craig said. "I'm going to clean up and head back to Boston." He stood for a moment longer, his eyes unfocused, his body swaying slowly and then with a deep sigh he seemed to realize what he was doing and he shook his head.

"I'm sorry, I was day dreaming," he said, turning around, heading for the bedroom.

Paul looked at Lynn, and raised his eyebrow in a silent question.

"He'll be okay, honey," she said with conviction. "Remember, he is Andrew's son."

He nodded his head in silent approval, his eyes red-rimmed from lack of sleep. A few minutes later Craig was back, bag in hand, his face showing all the conflicting emotions that he was feeling.

"Call us when you get back," Paul said, getting up and facing Craig, shaking hands, "and I'll see you at the ceremony."

Lynn came to him and embraced him, kissing him softly on the cheek. "Take care of yourself, Craig," she said, holding him tightly then letting go and taking a step back.

Craig didn't answer, just fastened his eyes on them and slowly, like a man a hundred years old, he nodded his head and turned around, making his way out.

# 32

Boston, Massachusetts
11 May 1973

    Craig Barlow waited patiently for his grandfather to come down for his ritual morning walk. It was nine in the morning and he was on his third cup of coffee while waiting. He had returned from North Carolina late last night and had decided to stay at the mansion instead of going to his apartment and get into something with Barbara. He had not talked to her in several days and he knew she would be pissed. He wasn't ready for that, but knew that sooner or later he would have to face it, but not now. Now it was time to face his grandfather and he had a feeling that it would not be a pretty sight. He had been unable to sleep much, his brain tired and numb after all that had been going on. He had thought a great deal about his father, the word no longer strange to him and he had felt cheated somehow. He thought about his mother too, and the fact that she had probably never suspected the depth of involvement or the extent of her father's devious ways and he felt sorry for her. She had gone to her grave thinking that Andrew Beck had lied to her, had never written, and all the time her father had been conspiring to make sure that she didn't get any of his letters. He browbeat her until there was nothing left but a shell and she had finally conceded to his wishes.

He finished his coffee and got up, his eyes taking in the beautiful surroundings of the place. He had been sitting outside on the back porch, the place lined with stately imposing oak trees. Everything was green and the weather was perfect, a day to feel alive and at peace with the world.

He was engrossed in his thoughts when he heard the door to the garden opening and the figure of his grandfather stepped out, the door closing softly after him. He was alone, as usual. His grandmother, Susan, had been bedridden for several years now, suffering from some debilitating disease that the doctors never seemed able to diagnose, her mind deteriorating slowly.

Robert Weatherly, III, walked outside, his eyes registering surprise at the sight of his grandson waiting. He was seventy-one years old, his body not as erect, and his gait slow. His hair was almost gone giving his face an odd look, but the eyes were still clear and bright, as cold and penetrating as ever. He came to stand in front of Craig, his eyes showing irritation, wondering what Catherine's pup wanted now. They had never been close, Robert Weatherly refusing to have anything to do with him when he was a child.

I guess now I understand a lot of what had transpired with my father and him, Craig thought, glancing at his grandfather.

"I need to talk to you, grandfather," he said, the word almost choking him. Robert Weatherly looked at his grandson closely, something in the young man's voice and demeanor alerting him that whatever was coming wasn't going to be to his liking.

"Can't it wait?" he said, the irritation clearly heard in his voice. "You know I don't like to miss my early walk."

"Sorry, this can't wait," Craig said, his voice flat.

Robert Weatherly looked closely at his grandson, the eyes boring a hole through him and then he shrugged his shoulders.

"Well, if it can't wait…" he said, sitting down on the bench.

Craig cleared his throat and started. "I received a letter the other day," he said, his tone neutral now, "from the Pentagon, concerning a man by the name of Andrew Beck."

At the mention of the name Robert Weatherly looked up, his eyes hooded now, anger spreading on his face.

"I'm glad you remember the name grandfather," Craig said, seeing the reaction on the man's face. "He is dead, you see, and there will be a memorial service honoring him and the President of the United States will award the Medal of Honor to his survivor." He stopped talking, realizing that there was no enjoyment in this. The cold anger that had been his traveling companion was now gone, leaving him empty. With a sigh he continued, eager to get it over with.

"He died in Vietnam, defending the ideals that make this country great, answering the call of duty."

Robert Weatherly got up, his face red, contorted in anger.

"I don't care to listen to any more of this garbage," he said, attempting to push by Craig.

"Oh no," Craig said, blocking the way, his hand clasping the old man by the arm, his face inches from him.

"You are going to hear this if I have to hold you still while I'm talking."

"How dare you manhandle me, you…you bastard," Robert Weatherly sputtered, spittle flying from his lips.

"Shame on you grandfather, calling your own blood such names," Craig said, applying pressure to the arm, seeing the face register the pain and quit the struggle.

"Now, be so good as to hear what I have to say and then you won't have to worry with me anymore."

Old man Weatherly sank back on the bench, his face breaking into a sweat.

"I feel pity for you grandfather. You never bothered to find out who this Andrew Beck was, what kind of man, what he was capable of. The only thing you cared was that he was poor, not of the same class. And because of that you condemned my mother to a life of despair and pain, forcing her to marry a man she didn't love. And I never shared my life with him, the man whose blood runs in my veins." He stopped talking, seeing the emotions playing on his grandfather's face, waiting for some word, anything that would tell him that the old man was sorry. But it never came and he continued.

"You never gave him a chance, or my mother, or me," he said. "But you know what, grandfather? He was a man who went far with nothing but raw guts and willpower, a man whom I'll be proud to call father any time."

Robert Weatherly's head came up sharply, glancing at Craig. "What the hell are you saying young man?" he said. "Don't tell me that you are planning on announcing this crap to the world, letting everyone know that you have another father."

"Why not grandfather?" Craig said, noticing the glimmer in the old man's eyes. "Afraid of what people would say about your good name?"

"I'll erase your name from my fortune, young man, if you cross me on this," he said, rage clouding his face, the veins of his neck bulging. "Don't you dare, damn you, I'm warning you."

Craig fixed his eyes on the old man and he felt pity for the human being in front of him. The shallowness of the man was without end and he felt that he was not a part of this family anymore.

"That's not going to work with me, grandfather. I don't care about your money or your name," he said softly, all the anger gone now. "If you had a decent bone in your body you would realized that what you did was vicious and callused and I hope that one day you suffer as much as my mother did." With that Craig whirled around, leaving the old man stunned. The damn bastard was going to ruin his name anyway, he thought, his mind racing ahead, trying to find a way to sway what he knew was coming. A cunning light came into his eyes and his forehead wrinkled in thought. He stood still for a moment and then nodding his head to himself he started walking. He might just have the leverage that he needed after all, he thought, smiling at his idea.

# 33

Boston, Massachusetts
12 May 1973

    Craig Barlow made his way to his apartment early the next morning. He had avoided Barbara, feeling like he had to come to terms with his feelings once and for all before he faced her. Was he going to change his name? Or was he going to keep up the front and call himself Barlow. Was he going to honor the memory of his father or pretend that everything was just like it was before? That and a hundred other questions kept him awake at the motel room most of the night until daylight brought an end to his musing.

    He entered the apartment looking around, finding the bed unmade. Barbara was nowhere in sight and that was odd. It was too early for her to be up and Craig wondered where she could be. He fixed coffee, sipping it slowly, watching the hands on the clock, waiting, but to no avail. Barbara wasn't coming. He was too restless to sit in the apartment and was on his way out when he heard footsteps on the stairs, Barbara finally appearing. She was dressed in jeans and a white shirt, sandals on her feet and she gave a small gasp when she saw him.

"Craig, you are back," she said, hardly any emotion showing on her face. Her green eyes had a hard, speculative look in them and Craig thought that he was in for a hard time.

"We need to talk," he said simply, holding the door open for her.

They went in and Craig didn't waste any time in getting to what was on his mind. He told her everything from the letter to what he had been doing for the past several days, watching for a reaction from her. Barbara remained silent, listening to Craig and when he finally finished she came to him, giving him a green-eyed stare. "This is overwhelming, Craig," she said softly, her hands touching his face in a caress. "You must feel confused and out of place, but you must remember who you are. You don't need to go to this stupid ceremony and in two weeks we will be married and out of here. No one will have to know that you have a different father than the one who raised you."

"What are you talking about, Barbara," he said, disengaging her hands, stepping away from her. "I'm going to this ceremony and I'm thinking of changing my last name, taking my father's name."

"Are you crazy?" Barbara asked, her voice cold as ice now, her eyes hard. "If you do such a thing your grandfather will see that you don't get a dime from him."

Craig heard her talking and then the pieces fell into place. She had been talking to his grandfather! The old bastard had summoned her, thinking that maybe she could get to him and make him change his mind.

"You have been talking to my grandfather," he said, the reaction in her eyes telling him that he was right. "I don't care about his damn money, Barbara. I don't need it, or his name."

She was silent for a moment, her face a mask, her forehead creased in thought and then she said, "You better think about what you are doing, Craig. I'll not be the laughing stock of this town just because you think you have to do the honorable thing. You might lose more than your grandfather's money. You might lose me." With that she whirled around, heading for the door.

"Wait a damn minute," Craig said. She stopped, turning around, her eyes smoldering, fixed on him.

"Don't you think that what I want is important? That my feelings concerning my real father have something to do with my decisions?"

She stared at him like he was an insect and then she spoke, "I don't care about your feelings or what this man represents to you," she said, taking a step toward him, her face hard. "All I know is that you are throwing away your name and your inheritance over some damn stupid notion that you have to do what is right." She stopped, looking at him intently and then she continued. "You do what you want to do but remember, I'll not be around to see you make a fool of yourself." She turned around and pulled the door open, slamming it after her, leaving Craig standing in the middle of the room, his head spinning.

He ran his hand through his hair, thinking about what had just transpired. To hell with what everyone wanted him to do, he thought, I'll do what is necessary to honor the memory of the man whose blood runs in my veins. He would go to the ceremony and after that he would see what course he needed to follow with his life.

# 34

Arlington Cemetery
15 May 1973

 Craig Barlow had been standing in front of his father's grave for well over an hour. He had never been to Arlington Cemetery before and was in awe at what he saw there. Row upon row of uniform headstones, as far as the eye could see of men and women who had paid the ultimate sacrifice for their country, for their freedom.

 With help from the staff he found his father's grave early in the morning and read the headstone.

    Colonel Andrew Beck, U.S. Army
    Born: 19 January 1927
    Died: 25 December 1972
     Republic of South Vietnam

 He had called Paul a couple of days before and received instructions about the ceremony. He had made his way early, wanting to spend a few minutes alone with the man he had never really known, his father. And here he was, feeling the warm sun on his back while his soul was cold as ice. He was standing at a small hill overlooking the Potomac River and the capital, the clouds rolling in a blue sky and the day warm and soft, perfect. He was engrossed in his thoughts when a touch on his arm brought him back and he looked around to see Paul Ragsdale and his wife next to him.

"I called your hotel room this morning and they said you were gone," Paul said, standing next to him. "I thought I might find you here."

Craig nodded his head looking back at the grave. "I needed to come and pay my respects, Paul," he said softly, turning back around to face his friend. Paul was wearing his class "A" uniform, his chest resplendent with medals, a Green Beret firmly on his head. Craig looked at them, realizing that he was beginning to recognize most of them.

"I understand, son," Paul said, a small smile on his face. Everything was going to be all right, he thought, watching the young man closely. He had feared that Craig would not show up, had said as much to Lynn, but she had just looked at him, telling him that he was crazy. And the boy was here.

Paul looked at his watch, noticing the time. "They will be getting here soon," he said watching the workers lining up the chairs, seeing several cars stop by. Chairs had been arranged close to the grave and a podium set up for the President. They went and sat down, watching the place fill with friends and comrades of Andrew Beck, and slowly the crowd grew until there were no more seats and people were standing. And still they came. Army officers and civilians, retired personnel and personal friends. Paul tried to keep tabs on who they were while talking to Craig, but he finally gave up, watching the throng of people silently coming to pay honor to one of their own. And then it was time, the motorcade bringing the President of the United States coming down, stopping and people getting out.

Craig looked at them, seeing the President emerge and then, to his surprise and delight he saw the dear figure of Uncle Henry step out of the car and his heart was glad. The President, with Uncle Henry at his side, made his way to the podium and eventually there was complete silence.

From somewhere behind them a band played the National Anthem and everyone stood up, facing the flag. After that there was silence again until an officer, a full bird Colonel, marched to the podium, coming to stand at attention next to the President, who looked at him, nodding his head in assent.

The officer brought a paper close to his face and he started reading, his voice strong, carrying clearly over the assembly.

Beck, Andrew
Rank and Organization: Colonel (then Lt. Colonel), U.S. Army 5th Special Forces
Place and Date: Loch Nin, 25 December 1972
Entered Service at: Stonewall, Texas, 1950
Born: 19 January 1927, Stonewall Texas
General Order 47:
Citation:

"Colonel Andrew Beck, (then Lt. Colonel), U.S. Army, 5th Special Forces Group, distinguished himself by showing great gallantry and intrepidity, above and beyond the call of duty, in action against hostile forces on 25 December 1972 in the Republic of Vietnam.

At approximately 1100 hours on 25 December 1972, a twelve-man Special Forces team had been inserted in the area of Loch Nin to effect a secret mission when the team met with heavy enemy resistance. Emergency extraction was requested by the team leader and after an attempt was made the helicopters returned to base, unable to land due to weathering small arms and anti-aircraft fire directed at them. Colonel Beck, the Detachment Commander, was monitoring the operation by radio when the call for extraction came in. He voluntarily boarded a chopper, returning to assist his beleaguered comrades. Upon arrival at the scene Colonel Beck jumped from the chopper at the same time the bird was hit by an RPG, destroying it. Colonel Beck killed the enemy soldier and ran to assist the crew, helping the wounded door gunner to safety, getting wounded himself in the process and again when mortar fragments exploded close to him. Despite his wounds Colonel Beck ran to where the rest of the team was pinned down, taking charge and directing the survivor's fire to where it would be most effective. Noticing the undefendable position they were in, he instructed the men to move and he dragged and carried several of the wounded to a defensive perimeter next to the downed aircraft, getting wounded in the leg during the process. On his second trip with the wounded men and while at the perimeter directing artillery and gunship fire at the enemy, grenade fragments hit him in the arms, face and chest. Refusing medical help, he mustered his strength and called for another extraction helicopter. Popping smoke when the chopper was close by, directing the beleaguered team to fire in order to facilitate the extraction of the wounded while the Med-Evac was down, he returned one more time to carry the dead team members back. On his third trip he was mortally wounded, this time in the chest, killing the enemy soldier who had shot him and getting the last dead American back to the defensive perimeter before he collapsed.

Colonel Beck's superb leadership, indomitable courage and consummate devotion to duty helped save the lives of at least ten men. His courageous actions in the face of overwhelming odds reflecting the utmost glory upon himself and upholding the finest traditions of the United States Army.

"The Medal of Honor, second award, is hereby awarded posthumously to Colonel Andrew Beck, to be received by his only survivor, his son Craig Beck."

The officer finished reading and then he walked in front of Craig, his mouth inches from his ear. Craig nodded his head at whatever was said and got up, coming to stand next to the President.

The President of the United States cleared his throat and looked slowly at the crowd assembled there and then he spoke.

"Ladies and gentlemen, we are gathered here today to pay tribute to an American hero, a man who by his actions and his unselfish devotion to duty exemplifies the best that America has to offer."

"Colonel Beck was previously the recipient of the Medal of Honor and if I read you his citation today it would read something similar to the one you have just heard." He was silent for a moment and then gathering his thoughts he continued. "He was a man who lived by a simple code of honor. Words like God, country, and devotion to duty were the primary forces that moved him, those were the words to live by and in the end, words to die for."

He was silent again, gazing at the crowd and then he continued.

"I'm sure that if Colonel Beck was here today and we asked him why he jumped in that helicopter to go and attempt to rescue his fellow soldiers he would tell you because it was his duty and the right thing to do. He didn't have to go and face a possible death at the hands of the enemy, but he went anyway, and by doing so paid the ultimate price, giving his life for his fellow man."

"Words alone can't testify to our feelings for such a man and his actions. His loyalty and courage, his determination and indomitable faith against overwhelming odds, make him a proud representative of our nations best, the ones who always give the last drop of their blood for a cause or for an idea in order that our nation stay free."

The President stopped then, the Colonel approaching, a small case in his hand. The President took it, opening the lid and extracting the Medal. He turned around, facing Craig and solemnly put the Medal of Honor over his head and around his neck, taking a step back and saluting. Craig looked at the man in front of him, his throat hurting with the force of his emotions and he returned the salute, seeing the President smile. He lowered his hand and the mournful notes of Taps started playing, the haunting notes sending chills through Craig's body, the tears brimming in his eyes. He felt a hand on his shoulder and turned to see Uncle Henry next to him, his eyes also wet. He lowered his head, emotions overwhelming him and finally in that moment the young man who was Craig Barlow came to terms with who he really was. He was the proud son of a soldier, a man called Andrew Beck and his blood ran strong in his veins. Among the tears streaming down his face he smiled finding the peace for which he had been searching for so long.

When Taps was finished the President once again turned toward the officer and a folded American flag was handed to him and in turn handed to Craig. The President saluted one more time and then it was over, the crowd coming to him, Uncle Henry wiping his eyes and smiling at the same time. He saw Paul and his wife, Lynn, both crying and he wondered again at the depth of the feelings his father had been able to inspire among his friends. He shook several hands, the names of people crowding his head until a tall ramrod straight man in civilian clothes stopped next to him. The man had kind eyes and a pencil line mustache on his lip. He smiled ruefully at Craig, extended his hand, and introduced himself. "I'm General Devlin, son, and I had the pleasure of knowing your father when he was about your age." He paused, pulling a cigar from his pocket, his face breaking into a smile. He lit and puffed on it, fixing his eyes on Craig one more time. "We served together in Korea and I was here when he was awarded the first Medal. He was quite a man son, quite a soldier." His voice was soft, sad even and his eyes seemed to be a thousand miles away until he smiled one more time and then he said, "If you are half the man Andrew was we expect great things of you."

He stopped then, standing at attention, snapping a salute to the flag and the Medal and then he whirled around and was gone, leaving Craig with his mouth open. "What was that all about?" he asked Paul, now at his side.

"That was your father's mentor and friend, Craig," Paul said, smiling. "Major General (retired) Devlin. He was our commanding officer in Korea and then again when Andrew worked for him for a brief period before joining Special Forces."

They shook hands with more people until the place was almost empty and then Paul reached inside Lynn's handbag coming out with a dirty, sweat stained, Green Beret, a silver leaf denoting the rank of Lt. Colonel pinned on it.

"This was Andrew's beret, Craig," he said. "He was wearing it when he died in Vietnam. I'm sure that you would like to have it."

Craig stared at the Green Beret, wondering how many fights, how many hours of danger and peril that green piece of cloth had gone through on his father's head. He glanced at Paul, his father's best friend, more like a brother and he could see the pain still deep in his eyes and he saw the two of them, smiling at the camera, together always, sharing the good times and the bad. And he made his decision. As much as he wanted to have it he knew that Paul was the right person to keep it, the one who deserved it the most.

He shook his head no and then he said, "You keep it, Paul. I know he would have wanted you to have it."

Paul nodded his head in assent, unable to speak, emotions welling up inside him. Slowly, carefully he folded the beret, putting it back in the handbag.

"Are you ready to go?" Paul asked, fixing his eyes on Craig.

"No, not yet," Craig answered.

When the place was completely empty, Craig glanced around and with a determined look on his young face he walked toward his father's grave. Paul and Lynn saw him go and they stood still, waiting. They saw the young man stop, his head inclined like in prayer and then, they saw his hand touch the headstone briefly. After a few seconds, Craig turned around and approached his father's friend, an apologetic look on his face.

"I'm ready now," he said simply. Paul grinned and nodded his head at him. Slowly they exited the cemetery, each one lost in their thoughts while the wind whispered among the headstones in that most hallow of places and the soul of those who gave their life for God, country and freedom rested in eternal peace once again.

# 35

Boston, Massachusetts
16 May 1973

Craig stood at the entrance to the old mansion, his hands jammed in his pockets, staring at the beautiful view offered by the countryside. It was a warm day, the sun shining bright, a slight breeze ruffling the leaves on the trees, making the day pleasant and bearable. Next to him were Uncle Henry and old Benjamin, while Carlotta stood by the open door, a sad look clearly visible on her face. Craig had returned to his apartment to find it empty, the furniture gone and everything that belonged to Barbara was missing. At first he was confused and then he found the note telling him that she couldn't marry a man who was so stupid as to throw away a fortune and on and on, until Craig had thrown the note away in disgust. The damn woman was after nothing but money and social standing, he thought, smiling inwardly. She doesn't know that I don't need my grandfather's money, that I am independently wealthy from the trust funds from my mother and my uncle. He had looked around the place one last time, his mind all made up about the future. Finally he had packed his bag, closing the apartment and heading for the mansion. He had talked to Uncle Henry about his plans and had seen the smile creep upon his Uncle's face, his head nodding in agreement, thrilled at what he had heard. The boy had guts, no doubt about it, Henry had reflected at the time, doing what he thought was right regardless of what his grandfather wanted. The young man had changed in the last few days and Henry thought it was for the best. It was like he had matured and there was confidence and pride etched on his face. He stood taller and the eyes were clear, full of life.

And today he was leaving his mind all made up. The firm lawyers would take care of the paperwork concerning the changing of his last name and Uncle Henry had promised to keep after them until it was done. He had said his goodbye and was looking at the old place wondering when he would see it again, when he was jolted out of his reverie by the sound of an incoming car. He looked up to see Barbara's sport car barreling up to the house. She stopped in front of them, the tires loud on the gravel, getting out, showing her well-tanned legs encased in brief shorts. She looked great, Craig thought, glancing at the beautiful woman, wondering what she wanted after just three days.

She came up to him, saying hello to Uncle Henry, ignoring Benjamin and Carlotta and then she said, "I want to talk to you Craig, alone."

Craig looked down at her standing on the steps and shook his head no.

"Whatever you have to say, say it. This is my family."

She looked around seeing the traveling bags and the Corvette in the driveway and her expression was puzzled.

"Going somewhere?" she asked.

"Yes I am," Craig said. "I was just about to leave." He stepped down and around her, really not interested in what she had to say. He had had enough of Barbara, realizing that beyond her beauty there wasn't much substance to her.

"Wait," she said, agitated now. "I don't want you to leave, Craig. We are getting married next week and… I didn't mean a word I said before."

Craig looked at her, something like disgust etched on his face and he walked down the remaining steps. He stopped at the car door and turned around to look at her. He glanced up at Uncle Henry who was looking at them expectantly.

"I'm leaving, Barbara. And there is not going to be any wedding, not next week or ever." Saying that he turned, opened the door and threw his bags in. He glanced at her, noticing that she was standing close to him, her arms on her waist and a hateful look on her face. A short, sad smile crossed his face and he fixed his eyes on hers.

"It's too late for this now, Barbara," he said, getting in the car. She ran to him, yelling.

"You can't do this to me, Craig, come back here immediately."

"I'm going away, Barbara," he said, "to answer the call of duty."

And with that he started his car and was gone, his past receding in the rear view mirror, the future wide open in front of him. He was going to be a soldier, the best he could be, just like his father before him.

For God, for country, for duty.